The Surge

ADAM KOVAC

Engine Books
Indianapolis

Engine Books
Indianapolis, IN
enginebooks.org

Also available in eBook formats from Engine Books.

10 9 8 7 6 5 4 3 2 1

ISBN: 978-1-938126-41-3

Library of Congress Control Number: 2018966237

We are, in short, a long way from the goal line, but we do have the ball and we are driving down field.

—General David Petraeus, 2007 Letter to the Troops

CHAPTER ONE

THE CORPORAL'S NAME WAS Larry Chandler and he was 23 years old. He sat on a folding stool in the building, smoking a *Gauloise* in the darkness. Outside the second-floor window, the nighttime wind swept across the desert. Moonlight reflected off the oil-stained highway that cut through the scrub grass and sand. When two headlights from a sedan appeared in the distance, he cupped the cigarette in his palm to hide the burning end and held it low between his knees. He waited for the car to pass. But the sedan coasted to a stop in front of the building. The high beams turned off and the taillights flashed as the car was shifted into park. He crushed the cigarette under the sole of his suede boot when three men stepped out of the car and stretched in the heat.

"Load your grenade launcher," Chandler said.

"Got a round in the pipe," said Hector Vogel, the soldier who sat next to him.

"They could be taking a leak," Chandler said.

"No," said Vogel. "These fuckers are dirty."

Chandler squinted through his night-vision goggles. In the lime-tinted glow, the sedan was the size of a child's toy, the shapes of the men dark and blurred. Vogel was built like a rhino and his silhouette loomed in the darkness. The big man raised his carbine with the grenade launcher mounted underneath to one of his broad shoulders and trembled faintly.

"Let me pop a flare," he said. "They'll shit themselves."

"What are they doing?" Chandler said.

"Standing," said Vogel. "Talking."

Chandler's goggles were mounted on the front of his helmet and tied to his ammunition vest with a long strand of parachute cord. He reached behind his ears for the buckles of the chinstrap and cinched tight until the goggles were closer to his eyes. He turned the lenspieces and adjusted the focus. Now, the men who'd gotten out of the sedan stood beside the open trunk. Two wore wool *dishdashas* popular with many Arabs. The third man, in a leather jacket and jeans, unloaded a shovel, a toolbox, and a heavy bundle shaped like a sandbag. Then they all squatted and huddled close in the soft sand at the edge of the highway, roughly two hundred and fifty meters away.

"They're planting an IED," Chandler said.

"No shit. Let's cap some Hajjis," said Vogel.

"That's not the plan," Chandler said. "And the road's too far. If we don't drop them in one volley, we'll be in a jam."

"I can still lob a few rounds out there."

Chandler's assault pack with the radio was by the window ledge. The long folding antenna extended outside. He pressed the handset against his lips and squeezed his gloved fingers around the transmitter and held it a moment before he called the gun trucks.

"C'mon," said Vogel.

Chandler listened to the static in the handset. He counted to twenty and tried again.

"They'd have answered by now," said Vogel. "It's broke. Or no one's listening."

Chandler swung the goggles above his helmet and removed his protective eyeglasses. He blotted the sweat on his sun-bleached eyebrows with a sleeve. His black and gray camouflaged uniform was damp and dingy and clung to his arms. The time was about 0200 and the temperature was in the mid-90s. But the concrete building had baked in the late May sun and now even hours later it was fifteen degrees hotter inside. Chandler thought about the sedan and the men on the highway. He licked his lips. Thirsty.

"We gonna sit here holding our dicks?" said Vogel.

"I'll switch channels," Chandler said. "Go wake up the other two."

Vogel swung his own night-vision above his helmet. There was a dull creaking as he shuffled on his stool. Then he lowered slowly to the floor and backed away from the window on his knees and elbows. "This is total gayness," he said.

"It's not your call," Chandler said.

"Those Hajjis will get away," said Vogel. "And someone's gonna get blown the fuck up."

After he'd gone, Chandler attempted to radio the gun trucks again. He hunched his long torso forward on the stool with his elbows on his knees, trying to ignore the flies and the air that smelled of manure. The heat and darkness thick like tar. Chandler waited. No one answered. He figured the rest of his squad had hidden in a *wadi* somewhere out in the deep desert, where they'd be unable to see the building or the highway.

He was thirsty because he was afraid. Before the sedan stopped, he'd been nervous, but mostly he was bored and lonely, sitting in the pitch black with three soldiers he'd first met that afternoon. Now he was frightened and the fear left his mouth dry, like sucking on a lump of chalk. Chandler thought about opening his pack to swap the radio battery, but he didn't want to take his eyes off the men on the highway. And the pain made it difficult to think. Chandler massaged his shins, peppered with flecks of metal and plastic from when he'd been wounded three years earlier.

"Jesus Christ," he said.

His assignment was to watch the highway. The Mehdi Army laid bombs and waited for the supply convoys headed north after refueling at Camp Tucson. The bombs rarely damaged the armored caravans. But lately the insurgents had gotten lucky. If they were quiet, a fire team could set up an observation post in the empty building, four kilometers from the camp in the desert of southern Iraq. And wait. When it was time, radio the soldiers in the gun trucks, who'd radio operations, and they'd relay the coordinates for the attack drone. Chandler thought it was a bad plan. An unnecessary risk for a unit rotating home in five weeks, and like most of what he'd seen so far in Iraq, it didn't make much sense. He didn't like any of it. Neither had his men when he explained it all to them earlier that morning in the trailer where they lived on the camp.

"Can't we shoot them ourselves?" Ted Gibson had said. He was pale with freckles and ice-blue eyes and leaned a bony shoulder on one of the wall lockers that divided the cramped, fiberglass box. A cigarette burned between his long, cracked fingers, the nails caked in grime.

"Self-defense," Chandler said. He tapped the laminated map against the pistol holster on his thigh. "We let the drone do the dirty work. The captain was serious about that."

"More glorified guard duty," said Vogel, who had tan skin and thick blonde hair shaved high and tight on the sides. He'd dismantled his carbine with the grenade launcher and his pistol. The pieces were spread neatly on his blanket. He sat shirtless in a canvas chair beside his bunk, in running shorts and sandals, rubbing the weapon parts with an oily rag.

"Switch with someone else," Chandler said.

"Right." Vogel slid the bolt into his carbine and racked the charging handle. Stacked high around his bunk were plastic milk crates from the chow hall to store his library, paperback Westerns and spy thrillers and classics, how-to manuals on car repair and cooking, even a few high-school texts, all stolen from the Red Cross tent. A White Sox pennant hung from one of the crates and swung in the air-conditioned chill.

"*Kurwa*," said Walter Witkowski. "We're too short for this." He tucked a snapshot of his wife and four daughters into the pocket of his cap. He groaned, lifting his short, round body off his bunk. He stood and stretched, scratching his bald, sunburned head. Then he urinated in one of the empty water bottles stashed beneath the wooden bed frame.

Chandler looked away. He tried to size up these men. Each held the rank of specialist. And even though the pair of stripes on his chest gave him authority, their monthly paychecks were the same. These soldiers had spent most of the tour in a guard tower, fighting boredom instead of insurgents. He wondered how they'd hold up in a jam. "All of you are National Guard?" he said.

"Volunteers," Gibson said. "From all over. 'Special unit for a special mission.'"

Vogel pushed a metal brush through the barrel of his pistol. "Nine months of this bullshit and no one's fired a shot," he said.

Chandler shrugged.

"I've seen this building," Witkowski said. "From the watchtowers. No one goes there."

"Not even the locals?" Chandler said.

"Never," said Witkowski. "And we're only going because someone wants a feather for his hat."

The trailer was quiet but for the air conditioner and the metal clang of a Zippo, which Gibson snapped open and shut with a greasy thumb. He and Witkowski stared at the floor. Vogel examined the veins in his thick arms. Then he smiled at Chandler and slowly did bicep curls with a full five-gallon water jug.

The radio set was atop bed sheets coiled in wrinkled lumps on one of the bunks. Chandler switched it on and put the handset to his ear. He keyed the transmitter and listened to the static.

"Sergeant Parker," said Gibson. "That girl at the commo shop. She says it's good to go."

"What took so long?" said Vogel.

"Have you seen Parker?" Gibson said. "Had to make a pit stop in the port-a-john."

Gibson winced and batted his hands as Vogel sprayed him with Febreeze. Afterward, he still reeked of diesel fuel, old cigarette butts, and feet.

"All American division," Witkowski said. He reached out and touched the 82nd Airborne combat patch on Chandler's right sleeve. He ran an index finger across the tab. "Wish we were getting one like that. You're the replacement they told us about."

"Thought I was finished playing Army. Went to college," Chandler said. "Studying for mid-terms when I got my recall orders. Deployed day after the Super Bowl."

"Heard stories about you," Vogel said. "Some kinda war hero. Walks like a gimp."

"Don't call me that," Chandler said.

"Guys like you can't stay away," said Gibson. "Being downrange, guess it's kinda like smoking crack."

"I didn't have a choice," Chandler told him.

Back on the highway, the three men still huddled behind the sedan. They'd dug a hole in the sand and placed the bundle inside. Chandler laid his carbine across his thighs. The M-4 was a cut-down version of the old M-16 rifle. His had a red-dot optic mounted above the receiver. An infrared laser latched and taped onto the barrel behind the front sight. He slowly removed the magazine and swapped it for one loaded with tracers.

The road's too far, he thought. You won't hit them.

Chandler listened to static in the radio handset. He breathed and his heart beat fast against the heavy chest plate in his body armor. He felt in his pants pocket for the whistle. He'd taken it from a dying man and since he'd returned from Afghanistan it was always with him. Then he lowered his night-vision goggles and adjusted the focus. The three men behind the sedan looked as if they were attaching wires to the bundle and a small box when Vogel crawled back to the window.

"These ass clowns aren't changing a tire," Vogel said.

Gibson and Witkowski knelt at the other window. They aimed their weapons at the road.

"The drone?" Witkowski said, leaning his weight against the stock of his automatic rifle.

"Working on it," Chandler said.

"They'll be done soon," said Gibson.

Chandler spoke into the handset. Static.

"That girl told me it was good to go," Gibson said.

"Shut up," Chandler said. "Trying to think."

"If they're planting an IED," Witkowski said. "We need to shoot them."

"Fuckin-A," said Vogel. He pulled up his weapon and thumbed off the safety.

"Wait," Chandler said.

The bundle in the sand exploded. Heat and sparks spat into the night. The three men and the sedan were swallowed by the brightness that erupted from the ground below them. Chandler groaned and lifted the goggles away from his eyes. He saw his silhouette cast onto the walls in the instant before he was blinded by the glare. The explosion sent a shockwave across the desert. Chandler felt a thunderclap and a violent rattle deep in his chest. When he could see again, Chandler blinked hard several times then lowered his night vision. Scattered around the sedan were scraps of flame. The burning debris glowed like coals before dwindling in the haze of dust and vapor on the highway.

"They blew themselves up," he said.

"Holy fuck balls," said Vogel.

Chandler had dropped the handset during the blast. He reeled it back by the cable and held it against his ear. Now the radio worked. The soldiers in the three gun trucks had heard the explosion and asked what happened. Chandler squeezed the transmitter and told them. He told them to drive quickly to the highway.

"The drone never showed?" Witkowski said.

"An accident," Chandler said. "I'm positive."

Chandler looked behind him. Through the window, three sets of headlights had rounded the camp. The gun trucks cut across the desert towards the building. When the patrol finally passed, the vehicles swung onto the highway and stopped when their headlights and spotlights shone on the sedan and flaming wreckage.

Witkowski unfolded the automatic rifle's bipod and set the gun on the floor. He carried an expensive digital camera in his thigh pocket and he aimed it at the highway and began to shoot video. Gibson brushed dust from the back of his skinny neck then picked his carbine and assault pack up off the floor.

"Stay. They'll tell us when it's time," Chandler said.

"We could help," said Gibson.

"We can't help them," Chandler said.

"You don't know that," said Gibson.

"You'll understand when it's daylight," Chandler said.

Vogel took the night vision off of his helmet mount then stood and punted the helmet into the dark. There was a dull thud as the helmet bounced somewhere on the other side of the room. "What a fucking joke," he said.

Chandler laid the handset on his pack. He lit a cigarette and blew smoke out the window.

"Ask the guys by the car if it's a joke," he said. "You can't. They got blown to a cinder."

Then they were quiet. Chandler smoked. The stale French tobacco crackled as it smoldered. He looked through his night vision at the highway. The dim camera light showed the wrinkles on Witkowski's face as he held it close and scrolled through the pictures and video he'd taken. Gibson leaned his back against the wall beside the window, thumbing his Zippo as Vogel did push-ups on the rough, sandy concrete floor.

"Three Hajjis got blown to a cinder," Vogel said, standing and brushing the grit from his hands.

Quiet. Finally, one of the soldiers chuckled. Another giggled. Someone farted and then all three laughed and they were hysterical. Their snorts and gasps echoed loud throughout the hollow building. Chandler clapped his palm over his mouth and listened. His thirst was stronger. And now that his hands had stopped shaking he felt tired. He yawned then reached for the metal thermos in his assault pack. He unscrewed the lid and drank, swishing the cold black coffee in his mouth. His throat was tight and it was difficult to swallow. He lit another cigarette and cupped it between his knees and listened to the laughter, thinking.

CHAPTER TWO

THE SEDAN ON THE highway had been a taxi. A shattered sign with Arabic script sat tilted on the roof. Burnt streaks like claw marks gouged the peeling white paint on the doors. The trunk lid had blown off and landed in the median. The back half of the frame was charred black and smashed, as if clobbered by a boulder or a giant fist.

Chandler kicked shards of safety glass into the roadside sand. There was a hand lying in the northbound lanes. Fingers curled. A rod of bone showed from the dark nub at the wrist. The sun had risen and now it was hot and bright. The windless air stank of scorched rubber and hair. Quiet except for the hum of flies. He waved them off his nose and ears.

"Mehdi Army," Chandler said. "Probably from Basra."

Staff Sergeant Antoine Mackenzie nodded and ate a vegetable omelet out of a plastic bag. He was the squad leader, and had the long and lean body of a distance runner. He chewed another bite then stuck the long brown spoon upright in the bag and wiped his hand on the back of his pants. He reached into his cargo pocket and held out a metal dial numbered one to sixty.

"From an old clothes dryer," Mackenzie said. "They set the time and drive away."

"There were no convoys last night," Chandler said.

"How would they know?" said Mackenzie. "Some holy man told them to go out and kill Americans so that's what they tried to do."

Chandler shrugged and lit a cigarette.

"Don't go thinking Hajji's stupid," Mackenzie said. "He's not. He's clever but in a simple sorta way. My first pump over here, detained some fools who seriously thought we had magic powers. Like a pill we took that let us wear our battle rattle in all this heat. You get me?"

Chandler stared at the hand on the highway for a long time until he didn't want to look anymore.

"Woolly Bugger," he finally said.

Mackenzie chewed his omelet and waited.

"Bait," Chandler said. "A kind of fishing lure."

Mackenzie nodded. He turned the dial in his fingers then flung it sidearm. The dial skipped and spun, clattering like a stone along the cracked concrete roadway before it stopped beside the wreckage.

"Talked to first sergeant," said Mackenzie. "Wants to see you. In the orderly room, as soon as we get back."

Chandler took out another cigarette and lit it off the end of the one he'd been smoking.

"Sounded super-pissed," said Mackenzie. "Hard to tell with that guy, especially over the radio."

"They blew themselves up," Chandler said. "We didn't do anything wrong."

"Tell him that," said Mackenzie. "He's your buddy."

"First sergeant's not my anything," Chandler said.

He'd never been outside Camp Tucson during the daytime. Far over the Kuwait border, flame and smoke belched from the refinery stacks. Contrails of an airliner streaked through the cloudless blue sky. A sea bird strafed the wreckage of the sedan and banked east, above the mud-baked homes on the outskirts of the port of Umm Qasr.

The sand lay infinite in every direction. Stretching towards the horizon like a vast carpet of bloodless brown ash. And then there was the trash. The highway was cluttered on both sides with water bottles, Styrofoam boxes, MRE pouches, Pepsi and Red Bull cans.

Garbage tossed from the passing convoys that'd piled up in the four years since the invasion.

"Hajji got balls," said Mackenzie. "Never put an IED this close to camp before."

"Vogel thought he'd get to kick ass," Chandler said.

"Know he practically maxed his enlistment exam?" said Mackenzie. "Scores were off the chart. And still picked the infantry. Best soldier in Golf Company. And since mid-tour leave, the biggest shit bag."

"He's nineteen years old," Chandler said.

"You act like that at his age?" said Mackenzie.

Chandler laughed. "Not at all."

Chandler squinted. He looked at the desert and the car on the highway, waving off flies before wiping his sunburnt face and neck with a cravat. Beneath the body armor, his T-shirt was wet with sweat and clung to his shoulder blades. He wanted to drink something cold and tried to ignore the pain in his legs.

He thought about the sea bird flying towards the port. Chandler couldn't see or smell the water and even though it seemed far away he knew it was close. Home, near Union, Michigan, the people who owned or rented cottages and mansions on the lakes would've started to return. Smell of cut grass. Willow trees drooping low above the docks and jet skis slicing along the cold water and by Memorial Day speakers cranking out "Takin' Care of Business" until the beer was gone. The busy season at the Eton's grocery store and he wondered if they would've phoned and asked him to drive back from college in East Lansing on the weekends to help stock the shelves.

"Five weeks left," said Mackenzie. "The captain's almost out of chances to win a medal."

"He'll get one of us killed," Chandler said.

Mackenzie nodded and poked his omelet with the long spoon.

"Captain loves us," he said. "But he's also regular army. Loves his career even more."

"Then he should get a new one," Chandler said.

"And do what?" said Mackenzie. He laughed and ate his omelet. When he'd finished, he flung the bag and spoon onto the roadside trash. His cigarettes were in a pocket beneath a combat patch from the 1st Cavalry. He lit one and exhaled a puff of menthol and cocked his head at the gray concrete building.

"What do you catch with it?" he finally said.

"Catch with what?" Chandler said.

"The Woolly Bugger."

"Whatever you want."

Mackenzie grunted. He removed his protective eyeglasses. The lenses dark as his skin stained with dust and sweat. His left eye was bloodshot and twitched. He glanced up at the blazing sun and curled his upper lip. He puffed on his cigarette then flicked it into the pile of roadside trash and turned toward the sedan and the hand lying on the highway. Mackenzie closed his eyes. Then he unhooked the incendiary grenade from his ammunition vest and nodded at the wreckage.

"Burn that piece of shit," he told Chandler.

Chandler stood on the highway, thinking. This is bad, he thought. He wasn't tight with these soldiers, but he wanted them to survive. He'd also like to look back and say they'd won the war but it was more important that they survived. Now they were running missions outside the wire. They might have to fight. And he knew, from Afghanistan, that sometimes the only way to survive in a fight is if someone else gets killed. He wanted it both ways and didn't know if that was possible and that, too, was a very bad thing. He figured by now he'd be numb to all bad things. Numb like he'd felt after he was wounded. Before the nerves in his shins had healed. Before he felt the tiny shrapnel pieces grind against the tendons whenever he walked. I'm a magnet for the badness, he thought. The badness is lying right there on that highway. Chandler reached in his cargo pocket and uncapped the bottle of Motrin. He scooped two painkillers into his mouth and let the pills melt under his tongue.

He stood on the road for a long time. Then he picked the hand off the highway and carried it to the body bags covered in flies laid out beside the sedan. He unzipped one of the black plastic sacks. He looked inside then put the hand inside and zipped it shut before the flies returned.

"Thanks for giving us a hand," Vogel said. The three soldiers laughed and then they were quiet. They sat in the long, narrow shadow that extended off the wreckage of the sedan, drinking water and smoking, oblivious to the heat and stench.

Chandler lapped the car. The blast crater was smaller than he'd imagined. The bomb left a basketball-sized dent in the sand with dark pebbles around the rim. He thought about the bomb. Not one of the new explosively formed projectiles that made the soldiers afraid. He guessed this one had been a crude cocktail of chemicals and fertilizer and the charges from an ancient artillery shell or a landmine. He'd developed an interest since Afghanistan but he was no expert.

"Where's the third guy?" he said.

"Mixed in with his pals," said Vogel. "We got everyone to fit in two bags."

Chandler opened his cigarettes and flipped one out. The cigarette was broken at the filter, as were the eight remaining in the pack. He wadded the pack in his fist and lobbed it through the hole in the rear window and onto the back seat of the sedan.

"Drink water," said Witkowski.

"Let me bum a cigarette," Chandler said.

"You'll faint," said Gibson. "Drink something. There's water in the trucks."

"I don't want any," Chandler said.

The gun trucks had set up a cordon three football fields away. On the opposite side of the roadblock, the lanes were gridlocked with Iraqi cars and trucks. The jalopies had colored tassels hanging from the windshields and tin chimes strung like fringe around the bumpers. The drivers squatted in their robes outside the vehicles and boiled water for chai in brass kettles set atop the engines. Others held cell phones to their ears, talking and gesturing at the wrecked sedan and the soldiers.

Chandler thought about the men talking on their phones and who they were calling. Stay here too long, he thought, someone might shoot a rocket at us. He took the incendiary grenade and gripped it tight and hooked his index finger through the ring for the pin. He set the canister on the hood of the sedan, wedging it between the windshield and wiper blades. He pulled the pin out slowly and stepped back and shut his eyes as the spoon popped off. The chemicals inside the canister turned the grenade into a blowtorch. The heat melted through the hood and engine block and ignited the fuel injectors.

The painkillers made his legs warm and limp. He was tired and it was hard to keep from falling. He opened his eyes and looked at the tall swirl of tangerine heat and flame devouring the sedan. After a few minutes, black smoke drifted in a haze across the highway. Steel belts visible on the tires as the rubber treads burned away. He stood and watched until a hand touched him on the elbow.

"We should go," Witkowski said.

The patrol left the highway and drove in a column across the desert. A typhoon of dirt splashed onto the last gun truck. The sand and hot glow of the morning sun rained inside from the turret hatch and swirled throughout the armored cab.

The air vents pumped dust onto Chandler's seat behind the driver. He lowered the cravat covering his nose and mouth. He bit the fingertips of his glove, pulled it off, and opened the ice cooler lashed to the metal boxes of machinegun ammunition beside him.

"Stay out of there," Sergeant Phillip Lazlo said. "There's only one left."

“I’ve been out in the desert,” said Chandler. “You rode in an air-conditioned truck.”

“Sucks, doesn’t it?” Lazlo said.

Chandler swished his hand inside the cooler. The melted ice water was cold and burned the cracked skin on his hand. He pulled a dripping can of grape soda from the bottom and rolled the can across his cheek. He dabbed two wet fingers at the grit in the corners of his eyes then pressed them against his clogged nostrils and sniffed the water drops until he could breathe again.

“What I just tell you?” said Lazlo. “There’s a case of water on the floor.”

The thought of drinking water made Chandler ill and sad.

“You owe me,” he said.

“Goddamn it,” said Lazlo.

Chandler popped the tab and opened the soda can and drained it in three swallows. He dropped the can onto the floor with the others and covered his face with the cravat again. His throat was dry and raw but there only was water left to drink.

“Still got that relic?” Chandler said.

Lazlo turned in the front passenger seat. He held a bayonet for an AK-47. Lazlo removed the bayonet from the scabbard. Daylight through the windshield reflected off the blade. Polished and honed since Chandler had last seen it.

“Spoils of war,” Lazlo said. “I’ll hang it in my living room.”

“That kid was maybe fourteen,” Chandler said. “He wasn’t going to hurt anyone.”

“Then why’d he hide it?” Lazlo said. “You know I hate frisking Hajjis.”

“He was a *Bedouin*,” Chandler said. “Used it to skin goats. I promised he’d get it back.”

“And I promised my boys a souvenir,” Lazlo said.

“That’s real nice,” Chandler said.

“Isn’t it?” Lazlo said. “And it’s not for sale.”

The haze around the gun truck cleared. The patrol slowed to

pass through the gap in the razor wire surrounding Camp Tucson. Plastic trash blown over the desert from the highway hung in shreds from the fence. Torn bags hovered on the wind like ghosts. The vehicles drove alongside a tall, earthen embankment to the main entrance gate. The column turned and traversed the concrete blast walls and sand-filled Hesco barricades stacked in a snake-like tunnel, past the sandbagged guard shack where Chandler had been assigned to work with Lazlo four months earlier.

Finally, he felt like a field soldier again. He'd gone on a mission outside the wire in full battle rattle, like the infantry were supposed to do. Dangerous but no more so than being on the camp, where soldiers were killed in accidents, beaten and raped by the Ether Bunny, blown away by someone carelessly cleaning a weapon. Chandler coughed in the dust, thinking of this and how much he still wanted to return to the camp and get out of the gun truck. He could ignore Lazlo, the sand, the heat, and the tiny rear seat. He wanted to be out because riding in gun trucks made him feel like he was locked inside a rolling metal coffin.

"Hook us up with pictures," said Lazlo.

"Pictures of what?" Chandler said.

"The dead Hajjis," said Lazlo. "All blown up and shit."

"Could've looked yourself," Chandler said.

"Too dangerous," said Lazlo. "I don't get out of the truck."

"Then use your imagination," Chandler said.

He thought about the men who'd blown themselves up on the highway. Misshapen body bags side by side in the bright morning sun. The hand on the road and what he'd seen inside the body bags made him think about other men he knew. Laying in a wheat field in Afghanistan. The shredded clothing and gore. How then and now all looked so different but still so very much the same.

"Wanna make a trade?" Lazlo said.

"For what?" Chandler said.

"The bayonet," Lazlo said. "It's nice."

"Very nice. But I got nothing," said Chandler.

"Your first deployment," Lazlo said. "Bet you made out like a bandit. Know you did."

Chandler fingered the metal bracelet on his wrist, scratched from toying with it so much. The bracelet was painted red and he'd had it engraved: *Metal fragments in body. Do Not MRI.*

"Yup. I brought back a few souvenirs," he said. "But I don't think you'd be interested."

CHAPTER THREE

THE GUN TRUCKS PULLED alongside the clearing barrels and stopped. Chandler pushed against the armored door and climbed out slowly. He stood in the open hatch and grabbed onto the frame to keep from falling. The back seat was cramped and he'd rode with his knees bent into his chest and now his legs were asleep. He slapped the dust on his fatigues, coughing and waiting until the blood flowed before joining the others.

"Think about what you're gonna write," he told them. "The captain's gonna want a good explanation."

"That's your job," Vogel said. "All I gotta put down is: I sat all night in an empty building. It was hot. Three Hajjis pulled up in a car. They had an IED. The IED exploded. The Hajjis died. Thus ends my statement."

Chandler shrugged. He pointed his toes to flex the tendons in his shins.

"Go on," he said. "I wanna take a walk."

The patrol drove off toward the fuel point and the motor pool. The clearing barrels were for unloading weapons. Chandler stood beside them and watched the patrol. The barrels were fifty-five-gallon drums sawed in half and filled with dirt and gravel. He dropped the magazine from his carbine and stowed it inside the dump pouch on his ammunition vest. He pointed the muzzle of the carbine into one of the steel barrels and cocked the charging handle. Sand scratched loud against the buffer spring. He ejected the loaded five-five-six shell into his palm then drew his nine-millimeter pistol and unloaded that, too.

He strapped the carbine to his assault pack then swung the heavy pack with the radio inside onto his shoulders. He cinched down the straps and walked along the edge of the gravel footpath and into the camp.

He was limping by the time he reached the massive fiberglass dome housing the chow hall. At the replacement depot, he'd been issued the latest boots with running shoe soles that felt comfortable on flat concrete. But now he could feel the gravel grinding through the treads, scraping hard against the balls of his feet and heels. He limped on, past the PX and the barbershop trailers, the smaller trailers for the Java Shack and Hajji shop, the wood tables and benches under the large shade nets strung up on the edge of the basketball court. The mailroom. Operations, with the garden of satellite antennas planted atop the flat roof.

His shins ached and he knew they'd feel better after a rest. Chandler stopped at the long shacks for the Internet and telephone cafés and mounted a raised boardwalk. He opened the plywood door and went inside. He sat in a folding chair for a few minutes until his number was called then found a computer terminal close to the air conditioning and checked his Facebook and e-mail, massaging his legs until he could stand the pain.

He had one new message. From Bob Buggman. Chandler skimmed through his best friend's rambling for the important bits: Big party on the fourth at the lake house. The sublet hadn't trashed his room in their off-campus apartment. Girls everywhere. Buggman would be around for summer school because he was flunking two courses. Five cartons of Marlboros waiting on the kitchen table he forgot to mail. That he'd stopped by the lake to open up his dad's cabin and the Eton's grocery was closed. Heard old man Jim had been in and out of the hospital lately, but it was probably nothing Chandler needed to worry about. Don't get blown up again.

•

The queue for the Internet snaked outside the café. The soldiers and civilian contractors slouched against the side of the building in the painful sunlight. An outgoing supply convoy lumbered along the gravel road towards the exit gate. The armored semis towed fuel pods or flatbeds loaded with shrink-wrapped pallets of bottled water and boxes or metal shipping containers, headed for the camps and outposts in the north. Their escort vehicles from a company with the radio call sign Widow Maker drove alongside the convoy. Each vehicle in the platoon of gun trucks had a large black widow spider spray-painted on the forward turret shields. The armored side plating marred with the dark splatter of roadside bomb shrapnel or the linear bullet pattern of machinegun fire.

Chandler followed the gun trucks with his eyes and thought about where they were going.

Better you than me, he thought.

He walked slowly in the heat. The assault pack slung over one shoulder. He passed the gym and Red Cross tents then he made a shortcut between the rows of barracks trailers and the tents in the transient village. He thought parts of Camp Tucson looked like an interstate truck stop. A gypsy bivouac. A landfill. Colored beach towels and T-shirts dried on bungee cords. Power cables and hose strung up between the Hesco walls in a haphazard web. A thin tabby cat missing patches of fur scrounged among the flies inside an overturned trash bin. By the time he reached the maintenance bay and communications shop he was limping again. Chandler hefted the pack higher and veered to cross a huge gravel lot, the stones rutted with thick tire tracks, where the convoys staged after refueling.

The gun trucks from his patrol were parked in the motor pool outside the Golf Company supply and orderly rooms. The soldiers had secured the doors and hatches and steering columns with padlocks and chains before they left.

The wind began to blow. Gusts of hot sand swept over the long file of parked trucks. He thought about the e-mail from his roommate then he remembered when the foster agency placed him with the Etons the week he turned nine and they'd taken him to Lake Michigan to celebrate. The manic cries of the herons swooping out over the water, shrouded by the morning fog lingering at the edge of the breaking waves. How the August breeze flung sand off the dunes in hunks onto the long gray stretch of beach where he'd wandered barefoot and bare chested with a bucket and shovel, digging for treasure or artifacts and imagining what he'd do after unearthing sudden and enormous wealth.

She stood waiting for him on the wooden walkway that separated the supply and orderly room buildings. She was black, her skin darker than motor oil. She had large round eyes and wore sergeant's stripes and a floppy hat. A large knife dangled from her belt. His neck and throat warmed and he was tired and for a moment he didn't think she was real until he heard her voice.

"You the one with the bad radio?" she said.

Chandler read at the nametape on her chest.

"Sergeant Parker," he said.

"Whip it out," she said.

"Excuse me?" Chandler said.

"I wanna get this over with and I need to see it," Parker said.

"I don't think—"

"The fucking radio."

Witkowski hunched nearby on a bench built into the walkway. He rocked back and forward and wrung his knuckles in his lap.

Chandler unslung his pack and put it on the bench. He unzipped the main compartment and pulled the radio out and set it down on the walkway in front of Parker. He unbuckled his helmet and took it off and wedged his protective eyeglasses between the foam pads lining the shell. He could see her clearly now. Under the floppy hat, her head was shaved. Dark stubble showed beneath the brim, straight like tiny quills. A 4th Infantry combat patch. He breathed and his heart beat faster and he tried not to look at her but it was impossible.

"You crazy," she said. "Got your captain all riled up. Drug me out of my air-conditioned shop to fix this mess."

"It's not his fault," Witkowski said.

"Not talking to you," said Parker. "National Guard. Don't know nothing about commo."

"Inactive reserves," Chandler said.

Parker glared at him.

"I was recalled," Chandler said.

"Uh huh," said Parker.

"I'm not in the guard," Chandler said.

"Wearing corporal stripes, aren't you?"

"Yup."

"Then you ought to know."

Chandler found a pack of cigarettes he'd forgotten was at the bottom of his assault pack. He smacked the box against the heel of his hand before peeling off the wrapper. He stepped back and lit one and watched Parker crouch on her heels and inspect the radio. The way her fingertips turned the knobs then scrolled across the little rubber buttons on the keypad. She unscrewed the long antenna. Her lips pursed and she blew on the copper threads then wiped the threads against her thigh until they gleamed in the sun. She installed a fresh battery and lifted the handset to her ear, listening, milking the transmitter in her palm before unscrewing the cable and scrubbing the connectors with a pencil eraser.

"Radio's fine," Parker said. "What's the problem?"

"No idea," Chandler said.

"Not talking about the radio," Parker said. "You're limping. You get wounded?"

"That's how he walks," Witkowski said.

"Still not talking to you," Parker said. She stood and tugged the brim of her hat, veiling her eyes from the sun. She studied Chandler's smoldering cigarette and his sunburned nose, waiting.

"Bitten by a moray eel," Chandler finally said.

"You're not funny."

"I'm tired. Been a really long night."

Parker cocked her head and blinked. "Tell you what," she said. "Now on, you, and that means you Corporal Chandler, are gonna bring me your radios before every mission. Only way I can think of to keep this from happening again."

Chandler nodded.

"Then we're straight?" Parker said.

"Straight," Chandler said.

Parker took her carbine from where it lay against the bench. She slung it behind her back like support soldiers who carried a weapon only because they were ordered to, not because they planned on using it. Parker stepped off the boardwalk. She glanced back at Chandler then pulled the brim of her hat lower, leaning her narrow shoulders into the wind and blowing sand as she crossed the motor pool.

"She likes you," Witkowski said when they were alone.

"Where'd everyone go?" Chandler said.

"Vogel went to the gym," said Witkowski. "Gibson took one look at Sergeant Parker and said he had to use the latrine."

"Find them," Chandler said.

Witkowski rose from the bench and gathered up his weapons and battle rattle and pack.

"She likes you," he said.

"Then she's insane," Chandler said.

"Sexy," said Witkowski.

"Always the crazies," Chandler said.

"That's a bad thing?" said Witkowski.

"You don't know American girls," Chandler said.

"I am an American," said Witkowski. "I've been a citizen since I was seventeen and that was a long time ago. I'd other reasons for coming here."

Chandler nodded and patted him on the shoulder. "Then get me a coffee."

After he'd gone, Chandler squinted in the bright morning sun. He scratched the soft sunbleached hairs on the back of his scalp and dropped his cigarette butt into a rusted coffee can next to the orderly room door. He took off his body armor and ammunition vest and let the heavy gear drop on the wood planks beside the bench. He lit another cigarette and drew on it, exhaling slowly as he read the scratched lettering stenciled on the orderly room door. Chandler reached for the knob then stopped. Instead of going inside the office, he sat hunched on the bench and propped his elbows on his knees. He lowered his head and pinched the corners of his eyes, thinking.

CHAPTER FOUR

He was thinking about the day he was wounded in Afghanistan. The rain and November chill. His platoon had camped overnight inside a farmer's *qalat*. Beyond the walls lay fields of winter wheat and lush groves and mazes of irrigation ditches twisting in each direction across the vast bowl between the mountains. The distant white caps barely visible through the low hanging clouds.

Chandler sat in the shallow grave he'd carved for himself. He pulled his poncho liner tight around his shoulders and shivered. The morning drizzle stopped and soon the dull drone of rotors thumped above in the gray sky shrouding the plains. The Blackhawk landed in the field. Through his shooting hole in the mud wall, he saw the green wheat stubs fanned flat by the rotor wash, the paratroopers kneeling at the trailside, waiting for the signal.

"Lieutenant's finally going," said Chandler.

"Surprised he lasted this long," Doug Tran said from the next hole. He lay on his back. Arms folded across his chest. He shook slightly and stared at his breath.

"He was in a lot of pain," Chandler said.

"Man didn't want to quit," said Tran.

Chandler nodded and tried to ignore the cold, leaning closer to the small hole in the wall. Outside, in the wheat field, the paratroopers carried their platoon leader to the helicopter and slid the litter that bore him inside while another group unloaded the crates sent from the chow hall.

"Landmines," Chandler said. "Jesus Christ."

"Nobody died," said Tran. "And we're getting a hot breakfast out of the deal."

Chandler turned and looked behind him. The courtyard was empty except for the goat pen and outbuildings standing along the walls. He peered through the hole in the wall and when he turned again Sergeant First Class Neil Flowers stood there, rocking on the heels of his muddy boots. He'd approached the soldiers suddenly and quietly and now he regarded them with his narrow eyes.

Flowers pulled the war club from his belt and turned it in his hands. The club appeared very old. A large smooth round stone fixed at one end. Two feathers hung by the handle carved from a hardwood ash burl that'd been whipped with dark strips of rawhide.

"Found the Hajji latrine," Flowers said. He aimed his war club at one of the outbuildings.

"Thanks," said Tran.

"It's filthy," Flowers said. "Maybe someone, sitting around, smoking and joking, should clean it."

"Seriously?" Chandler said.

"As cancer in the third stage," said Flowers.

"What for," Tran said.

"A gesture. For our host. To win the hearts and minds."

Chandler shrugged out of his poncho liner.

"My gun's dirty," he said. Chandler charged the automatic rifle and lifted the feed tray and unloaded the ammunition belt. He jabbed a shaving brush at the dirt and grease gummed around the springs and pins. When he looked up again Flowers was gone.

"Hate that douchebag," said Tran.

The Blackhawk lifted from the field and banked over the walls as it rose into the clouds. It began to rain again. At first scattered and slow, then faster and harder and soon the sleeves on Chandler's uniform were soggy and heavy. He stopped cleaning and reloaded the belt and draped his Gortex parka over the gun. Raindrops dripped off the brim of his helmet.

The sound of the falling rain woke Sergeant Tim Reed, who

lay under a poncho in his hole. He sat up and stroked his moustache and glanced at the sky and the two soldiers nearby in the mud.

"You'll get pneumonia," Reed told them.

"Big chief snuck up on us again," Tran said.

Flowers squatted in the doorway of one of the outbuildings. He ate boiled noodles from his canteen cup with a set of metal chopsticks, studying the laminated map spread out at his feet.

"He's no Indian," said Reed. "Claims he's Chippewa because he knows you'll believe it and it'll mess with your heads. That gimmicky club he likes to wave in everyone's face, he ordered it in the mail."

"Scares me," Tran said.

Chip Dempsey arrived carrying paper plates with waffles and bacon and chicken thighs. Inside his cargo pockets were boxes of chocolate milk, Raisin Bran and plastic sporks. He doled out breakfast then sat and crossed his legs in the dirt between Chandler and Tran.

"Where's the juice?" Tran said.

"Not waiting tables here," said Dempsey.

"Fuck you, cherry," Tran said.

"Fuck yourself," said Dempsey.

They laughed then they ate in the rain and didn't talk. The waffles were frozen and the bacon was limp. The rain splashed and puddled in their plates, and watered down the sterilized milk they'd mixed with their cereal. Reed carried a folding tin stove and square fuel tablets he lit with a match. He took each of their canteen cups and heated water and mixed in coffee and cocoa and told them to drink.

Chandler held his cup under his chin to feel the warm steam on his face. He wasn't hungry and ate very little before he set his plate aside. The chill hurt in his bones. His uniform reeked of mold. He took off his helmet and sipped water from his canteen then doused his cravat. He cleaned the dirt around his eyes and behind his ears then he craned his neck, blinking against the cold falling rain and he sat like that for a long time.

"What's the plan?" he finally said.

"We'll patrol," said Reed. "Walk the fields. The villages. Walk back before it's dark."

"Did that yesterday," Dempsey said.

Reed took a bite of his waffle then flung it over the wall.

"Been walking almost a month," Tran said.

Reed nodded. He ran a tiny comb through his moustache.

"No action here." Tran said. "I wish we'd been sent to Iraq."

"Fallujah," Dempsey said. "Combat jump. That's what I'm talking 'bout."

"Nice," said Chandler.

Reed sifted the mud in his hands then he climbed out of his hole slowly and slung his carbine. He took a step then stopped and knelt and grabbed an uneaten chicken thigh floating on one of the plates in the rainwater. He squeezed the chicken thigh like a sponge until the juices dripped through his fingers.

"On the bright side," he said. "The chicken's juicy."

Reed walked to the outbuilding. The other squad and team leaders in the platoon gathered around Flowers and his map, talking in low voices. Tran watched them talking then cracked open his armored vest, reached in and unbuttoned the pocket of his shirt.

Tran held the whistle in his palm. The kind the drill sergeants all wore in basic training and the infantry school. Made of plastic that'd been dyed dark brown with a wooden pea inside. Through the loop was a length of black parachute cord, the ends burnt shut and tied with a clove hitch.

"Think he'll like it?" said Tran.

"It's perfect," Chandler said.

"We should wrap it," said Dempsey.

"In what?" Tran said. "We'll just fucking give it to him. Thanks for being a great team leader, Sergeant Reed. Good luck, smoke the shit outta them recruits, airborne and all that other happy horseshit."

Chandler nodded and spat in his hole.

•

The rain stopped at noon. A fire team and the mortar squad were left behind to guard the patrol base. The paratroopers charged weapons then shouldered their large rucksacks laden with ammunition and water and the bedraggled procession walked in a file onto the narrow path that led into the fields. Their khaki uniforms with the desert camouflage pattern and torn netting on their helmets clashed against the landscape of emerald wheat shafts and leaves.

They walked. They walked through the fields. Crossed irrigation ditches and streams of flowing muck and scattered stands of mulberry and poplars. They walked up then walked down low hills carpeted with high grass that rocked sleepy on the early afternoon breeze.

Two hours later the patrol halted and set security to search one of the walled farmhouses. They knew they wouldn't find anything. The rifles and rockets would be buried in caches hidden under rugs in the rooms were the women stayed and the American men couldn't enter. Outside, Chandler knelt in the dense grass on the edge of the path. He wrapped a wool scarf around his neck and shivered from the sweat cooling on his chest beneath his body armor. The wheat fields were empty except for a meandering dog with matted tawny fur and trembling legs that watched with its lone eye.

"Medieval," he said.

"You'd have loved Somalia," said Reed. "Termite mounds nine feet high."

"Hajji's got some mean-ass goats," Dempsey said.

"Bring me the goat," Tran said.

"The goat," Chandler said. "Bring it."

Reed lowered the binoculars he used to glass the fields.

"We ever take prisoners," Chandler told him. "We'll give them two choices: Tell us where Osama bin Laden's hiding."

"Or suck a goat's dick," Tran said. "Before you die, motherfucker."

"Die," said Dempsey.

They laughed and bumped fists and then it was quiet except for the wind rustling through the grass and the sound of their breathing.

The patrol walked for another hour, soaked boots scraping on the packed shale surface of the path. They stopped at the edge of another wheat field. Opposite the field stood more qalats not far beyond an irrigation ditch lined with willows. Flowers unfolded his map. He marked the location then pointed at Reed and motioned towards the ditch. Tran loaded a forty-millimeter shell into the launcher beneath his carbine.

"Douchebag," he said.

They fanned out and followed Reed through the field. Halfway across, Chandler swatted a large insect that flew by his ear. A low buzz as another flew past him, another and another. Then at once the field hummed like a furious hive and was filled with neon green javelins that streaked out from the ditch in long haphazard arcs. Chandler dove into the wheat shafts head first, like he'd been taught to steal second base. He put a hand on the top of his helmet and dug his nose into the mud. His mouth went dry when he realized the insects were not insects, they were bullets, and he didn't want to move because he'd never been shot at before.

Reed winced and crouched then fired three shots from his carbine and charged the ditch. Tran and Dempsey rose and ran after him. A clod of dirt burst beside Chandler. He got up and ran. The automatic rifle had a handle on the barrel and the gun swung behind him like a suitcase. He ran and his heart beat faster. Another clod exploded out of the mud. Chandler ran and thought he'd get hit before reaching the tree line and when he finally did he leapt through the twisted branches and across the ditch and pressed himself flat against the far slope.

Rainwater trickled though the bottom of the ditch. Tiny leaves lush on the bent branches above. Ankle-deep in the cloudy water were two bearded men. They wore stained dishdashas and camouflaged field jackets and as the paratroopers entered the ditch the men lowered their AKM rifles and turned and ran. Reed and Dempsey aimed their carbines and shot them in the back. The men splashed facedown into the brown water and were still.

Now they were being shot at from within the qalat beyond the trees in front of them, and from a grove across another wheat field bordering the walls. A tree exploded above, vomiting bark. Leaves flush with rain twirled into the ditchwater. Chandler shut his eyes and hugged the dirt when the second rocket-propelled grenade hissed through the foliage. The ground trembled when the rocket exploded in the field behind him.

His legs shook like when he was a seventh grader and the older boys would corner him at his locker and call him a dirty orphan and told him he better swing because they were going to kick his ass anyway. Chandler blinked and watched as Tran launched a grenade through a hole of rubble in the qalat wall. Dempsey reloaded then shot into the grove of trees. Reed was pointing and shouting but Chandler couldn't hear him. He breathed and licked his lips. He unfolded the automatic rifle's bipod and braced it atop the embankment and sighted at the puffs of gray smoke and flashes in the grove. He thumbed the safety and leaned forward into the stock. He squeezed the trigger, tightening his wrists to keep the weapon steady.

The tornado of noise hurt his ears. Chandler fired into the grove of trees, shifting fire to the qalat, then back at the grove. He emptied the two hundred-round drum magazine and two other drums he carried at his waist, firing left handed to yank the charging handle when the weapon jammed. He shrugged out of his rucksack and laid it on top of the ditch. He got out another ammunition drum and reloaded and kept shooting.

His eyes watered as gun smoke filled the ditch and wafted through the trees. An erection when the cordite stung his nostrils. He was afraid. But he didn't care if he lived or if he died. The blood surged in his brain, as if linking him through some ghoulish sacrament to the mud and the foliage, the other paratroopers and the Taliban he tried to kill. He wept and he laughed almost in rhythm with the automatic rifle pounding against his shoulder and he didn't care if he lived or if he died because he had never been more alive.

The balance of the platoon had advanced and joined them inside the ditch. Flowers stood at the bottom with his map, yelling over the noise into the radio. Then he gave the handset to the radio operator and climbed to the top of the ditch. Flowers stood at the edge of the slope and tree line. He howled. Green tracer bullets flew past but Flowers didn't flinch. He swung the war club over his head. The feathers on the handle circled like a carousel and he howled. He beat his chest and swung his war club, howling.

The planes finally arrived and bombed the grove of trees. The gunfire stopped. Chandler felt dizzy. Smoke rolled out the barrel of the automatic rifle and scattered beside it were the empty ammunition drums, metal links and brass casings from the belt. He listened to his heart beating.

Flowers sent two squads to clear the qalat then slid down and loomed above one of the dead men lying in the ditchwater. He studied the dead man for a long time, as if he searched for the solution to some complicated equation. Flowers raised his war club and he held it high for a moment then swung and swung again until he'd bashed the dead man's skull into four pieces.

Chandler watched this. Finally, he rose to his knees, took a long drink of water from his canteen then urinated and went to where Dempsey slouched against the slope. Dempsey bit his lower lip, fists shaking while he watched the medic bandage the frayed, cranberry stained nubs where his thumbs had been shot off.

"How's that even possible?" Chandler said.

Dempsey groaned and shrugged.

Tran waded through the crimson-colored ditchwater. He looked at Dempsey then stuck a finger into the smoldered hole in Dempsey's body armor. Tran pried a gnarled bullet jacket from the chest plate and showed him.

"You got lucky," Tran said.

"Go fuck yourself," said Dempsey.

A half hour they spent keeping Dempsey from succumbing to shock, nodding at the rifle shots and boom of grenades within the qalat while waiting for the helicopter to take him away. Chandler and Tran told him that he'd get his Purple Heart and Combat Infantryman Badge but at last he appeared to calm when they told him how everyone back in Oklahoma would buy him beers for the rest of his life.

The clouds had parted and sunlight shone on the wheat field. Chandler and Tran helped Dempsey climb out of the ditch and sat with him under the trees, waiting. Tran lit a cigarette and gave it to Dempsey, who held it between the pinky and ring fingers that stuck out from under the field bandages.

"See that shit?" Dempsey said. "What Flowers did to that dead Hajji?"

"Didn't see that coming at all," Chandler said.

"Someone finds out," Dempsey said. "He'll lose those stripes. Then go to jail."

"Maniac," Tran said. "Standing up in a firefight like that."

Reed stroked his moustache flat. He looked at his shaking hands and smiled then lit a cigarette and smoked it down to the filter in four drags.

"Not crazy," he said. "Gave the Hajjis something to shoot at. Didn't want them to bug out before the airstrike. Believes he's expendable. To a man like that, we're all expendable."

Tran shook his head. "Guy scares me."

The thump of helicopter rotors echoed across the fields. Tran draped Dempsey's arm over his shoulder and followed Reed onto the dirt and stalks of harvested wheat in the field where the Blackhawk would land. Chandler picked up Dempsey's carbine and rucksack and followed them.

"Feel woozy," Dempsey said.

"Keep walking," Tran said. "Last time I'm carrying your ass."

"Going to see the wizard," Dempsey said.

"Quiet," said Reed. "Or I'll get the goat."

"The goat," Chandler said. "Bring the goat."

"Suck it," Tran said.

"Before you die," said Reed.

They were laughing when Dempsey stepped on the landmine. A bright spark shot from the dirt. From the flash bloomed a black cloud and Chandler saw Tran and Dempsey vanish into the smoke and then Reed was gone, too, as if a phantom hand had snatched him away. The blast sucked the breath out of Chandler's lungs. He vaulted forward. Whooshing past was the dirt in the field and the trees along the ditch and the sunny sky and Chandler felt a snap in his brain when his helmet hit the ground and then he felt nothing at all.

Quiet. Chandler lay on his back and watched as the dark cloud floated over the wheat field and broke apart in the sky. He smelled blood. His pants and boots were ripped and peppered with marble-sized holes, as if mauled by an animal. He tried to stand but his legs were numb and stiff. Chandler shrugged out of his rucksack and rolled onto one shoulder and unbuckled his helmet and let it fall in the dirt. He breathed and licked his lips, eyes flickering across the short wheat shafts until he rolled over and began to pull himself forward with his fingers.

He followed the torn clothing until he found Reed and Dempsey. They lay side-by-side in a patch where the ground was raked bare by the explosion. Scorched uniforms stained black by the burning powder. The bodies busted open like piñatas. There was very little blood. Reed with white teeth gnashing, expression frozen in a wail, hollow gaze fixed on the fading afternoon sun, as if declaring to some higher power that there'd been a mistake.

Chandler looked. He was shaking and his eyes watered. Then he couldn't look anymore so he turned his eyes to the cut wheat stalks and mud in the field and stayed that way until he heard the faint blow of a whistle gargling somewhere in the field.

He dragged himself forward again. He found Tran sprawled sideways, the drill sergeant's whistle in his teeth, propped up on an elbow. One leg fileted from crotch to knee. Blood had trickled from his ears and was drying on his neck. Chandler coughed and tried not to look at the fist-sized hole in his groin.

"Larry. I'm all busted up," Tran said.

"I can help," Chandler said.

"Look at this bullshit," Tran said.

"Lemme see," Chandler said.

"Don't," Tran said.

He grabbed Tran's shoulder anyway and tilted forward him a few inches.

"Jesus Christ."

"I feel my guts sliding out of my ass."

"Lotta pain?" Chandler said. He unfastened Tran's body armor and removed his helmet.

"It hurts," said Tran.

"The doc's gonna come soon," Chandler said.

"No he won't," Tran said. "We're in a fucking minefield."

"They can fix this," Chandler said.

"What'd be the point," Tran said.

"You're pale," Chandler said. "Stay calm."

"Shoot me. In the head."

"Please be quiet."

"Then give me some water," Tran said.

"That might be bad," said Chandler.

"I want water," Tran said. "Give me water."

"Please. Stop talking."

"Everyone's dead."

Chandler nodded. The pain in his legs and feet and head made it difficult to see clearly.

"You're still alive," Tran said. "So gimme water."

"Please," said Chandler.

"Water."

He lay on his side in the dirt and listened to Tran. Chandler took the drill sergeant's whistle from him and wiped off most of the blood then he put it in his pants pocket. He lay there, listening to Tran. He squeezed Tran's shoulder and he tried not to look at him and after a while he couldn't listen anymore. Then he unscrewed one of his canteens and tipped the bottle to Tran's mouth and let his friend drink as much water as he wanted.

CHAPTER FIVE

CHANDLER SAT ON THE bench in Iraq, sweating under the blazing yellow sun. He massaged his shins then he stretched his legs and pointed his toes and rolled the stiffness from his ankles. The thinking had made him sleepy. Reminded him he was alone. He'd loved Tran and Dempsey and Sergeant Reed. He knew the love was different than loving family or a woman. But it'd been real and now it was gone and all he had left was the whistle. Maybe, he thought, if this tour somehow ended differently.

Windswept sand tumbled and curled along the sun-bleached walkway between buildings. Finally, he stamped the cigarette under his boot heel and flicked the butt into the coffee can. He stood and limped to the plywood door. He felt himself shake inside, but when he looked, his hand was steady. He read what'd been stenciled on the door before he turned the knob. Golf Company, Security Force Detachment. Gavin Ingram, Captain, Infantry, Commanding. Neil Flowers, First Sergeant.

A windowless office lit by long, naked bulbs wired to the ceiling. Each corner had a desk with a reclining chair upholstered in torn vinyl. Yellowed pages in binders stuffed onto tiers of metal filing shelves lining the walls. Everything coated in a thin film of sand and dust. Static hissed from a radio set cannibalized from one of the gun trucks and mounted on a long folding table. Packages and envelopes bearing stateside postmarks sorted into three piles. The room was chilled by an ancient air conditioner that coughed beads of water onto the floorboards. On the far wall hung a laminated map of southern Iraq. A dark line showed the highway twisting through the desert. Most of the overpasses and crossroads marked with red thumbtacks. Another red tack had been added to the map overnight, poked in the same grid square as the observation post and the exploded sedan.

Flowers sat with his boots propped on the corner of his desk. He pecked at a Styrofoam cup of instant noodles with chopsticks stained in a cherry finish and decorated with silver dragons and Mandarin *hànzì*. He smacked and sucked the noodles and looked at Chandler with his narrow eyes.

Behind the desk in the opposite corner was Roman Batista, swaddled in a fleece jacket. He hunched forward on a chair that'd had the arms removed to accommodate his six-foot-seven- inch hulk. Hands the size of Cornish hens, darning a wool sock. Batista looked at Flowers then at Chandler standing inside the door and he watched them watching each other. Finally, Batista laid his needle and thread on the desk blotter and eased back in the chair, twirling the sock.

"There he is," Batista said.

"Hi, shorty," Chandler told him.

"You're covered in dirt," Batista said.

Chandler nodded.

"Feeling alright?" Batista said.

"Been worse," said Chandler.

"You're walking funny again."

Flowers snorted and sipped broth from the cup. The room was quiet except for static on the radio, the air conditioner coughing, and Batista's thick fingers drumming on the desk blotter.

"I heard that IED go off," Batista said. "Orderly room vibrated. Thought, damn, second squad got in some shit. And then all the alert sirens went, awhoo, whoo, whoo, like back on the block when the prowlers roll up."

"You didn't miss anything," Chandler said.

Batista smiled. "I know that. I fight with a laptop."

Flowers slid his boots to the floor. He leaned back to drain the broth then placed the cup on the desk and rapped his chopsticks on the rim. "Shorty," he said. "Time for chow."

"I'm on a diet," Batista said.

"Then eat a piece of fruit," said Flowers.

"Haven't emptied the trash," Batista said. "And there's the duty log to fill out and my relief hasn't showed."

"Leave," said Flowers. "The corporal and I are going to have a chat."

Batista put the sock and sewing kit in the top drawer of his desk. He unzipped the fleece and draped the coat over the back of the chair. He straightened his cap, nodding at Chandler as he lumbered out the door, as if he'd realized he was late for something important. The door shut and the air conditioner coughed over the hiss of the radio static. Chandler slid a metal chair from under the banquet table and pulled it in front of the desk.

"I tell anyone to sit?" Flowers said.

Chandler froze in a squat then straightened up and folded his hands at the small of his back. He looked at Flowers, the lines on his forehead, the weight he'd gained since Afghanistan. The old war club lay among the memoranda and duty rosters covering the desktop. Flowers wiped his chopsticks with a handkerchief and stored them in a leather case and folded his hands in front of him.

"You're gimpy," said Flowers. "It's embarrassing."

"I'm driving on," Chandler said.

"Right," said Flowers. "Suppose you know the captain's disappointed."

"The radio locked up," Chandler said.

"That drone's expensive," said Flowers. "Unheard of for one to even be assigned to a unit like this."

"And then the IED exploded," Chandler said.

"I'm disappointed, too," said Flowers.

"I didn't think—"

"You think too much," Flowers said. He lobbed the Styrofoam cup across the room into the trash pail beside Batista's desk. The cup clattered atop empty cans of Red Bull, torn in half with the ends crushed flat. Flowers eyed the war club. He walked his fingers quickly across his paperwork like a spider then he looked up and over the desk at Chandler.

"Basic light-infantry tactics," he said. "Support by fire with your automatic rifleman and grenadier, maneuver with your rifleman. Engage in close combat. There's a manual around here that spells out how it's done."

"That wasn't the plan," Chandler said.

"You're a hero," said Flowers. "Act like one."

"Stop calling me that," Chandler said.

"Bronze Star. For valor," said Flowers.

"That I didn't deserve," Chandler said.

"People need their heroes," said Flowers.

"It's a sham," Chandler said.

"It's a war."

"Still a sham."

Flowers picked up the club and spun the handle in his fingers. He polished the big round stone against his shirt then adjusted one of the feathers before he set it down. He waved a finger at the chair. Chandler sat. Flowers opened a desk drawer and removed a pad of sick-call slips and a ballpoint pen.

"Sending you to the medics," Flowers said. "Finish the deployment in an office."

"I'm driving on," Chandler said. "Five weeks and a wake up."

"Might as well be a billion years," Flowers said. Static hissed through the radio speakers. The air conditioner sputtered then began to spit tiny chips of ice from the vents. Flowers glanced at the red thumbtacks dotting the map on the wall. "Especially if this company finds itself with a new mission."

Chandler thought about that. "What did the captain volunteer us to do?"

"Our jobs," said Flowers.

Chandler felt his mouth dry and he was very thirsty. He swallowed and pressed his palms flat against his thighs to stop the childlike shaking that rattled his boot heels on the floorboards.

"We guard the camp," he said. "This unit's National Guard and reserves, these guys aren't even real soldiers. No clue what they signed up for. They've got tombstones in their eyes."

"Then get a profile," said Flowers. "Tell the medics what happened last time. Take off your pants and show them your scars. The horror show. Be honest and tell them how bad it really hurts."

Chandler thought about that and listened to the ballpoint pen clicking open and shut like a metronome as Flowers watched him from the other side of the desk. "Not gonna quit," he finally said.

Flowers nodded. "A mistake. Don't know how it happened but they shouldn't have sent you here. You're not the only busted-up Joe who got recall orders in the mail. The troop surge, it changed all the rules."

"Don't mean nothing," Chandler said. He reached in his pants pocket and squeezed the whistle he'd taken from Tran in the wheat field. He looked at the war club on the desk and the red thumbtacks on the map. Flowers watched him for a long time, waiting, then shrugged and stood and adjusted his floppy cap in the mirror nailed to the inside of the door.

"We'll get new orders in a day or two," he said. "Think it over tonight while you're out in the observation post."

Chandler stood fast and it hurt.

"The position's been compromised," he said. "Mehdi Army knows we were hiding in there."

"Hope that radio works," said Flowers. "Captain Ingram's ambitious. Thought he might've gotten a Silver Star, using you guys to set the table so the drone could make a kill. Naturally, he thinks your squad dicked him over. I'm a first sergeant now, Chandler. I run this company. But I don't give the orders. All I can do is try to make this work. Remember, we're not in Afghanistan anymore."

Flowers left. Chandler sat and stared at his reflection in the mirror. He thought about things that'd happened to him in his life, the things he'd done and the things he hadn't. And he thought about the wheat field in Afghanistan. The air conditioner coughed and made a grinding noise and then it conked out. The air inside the office became hot and thick. Chandler reached in his pocket and pulled out the whistle. He sat and rubbed his thumb against the whistle then held it to his ear and rattled the small wooden pea inside.

"Not in Afghanistan," Chandler said. "No. We are not."

CHAPTER SIX

THE PATROL LEFT THE camp when it was dark and drove to the observation post. The gun trucks parked far away, along the edge of a deep ditch that snaked through the desert. The Detroit diesel engines idled as the soldiers climbed out and slammed the armored doors, talking. The gleaming cones from their flashlights swept over the sand and across the wall of the building, the windows and the doorway open like the mouths of caves.

Chandler and Mackenzie knelt beside the top of the ditch. They watched the three figures get out of gun trucks and walk in a crouch to the edge then lower themselves quietly over the side and slip into the darkness below.

"You got this?" Mackenzie said.

"Yup," said Chandler.

"Now's the time if you don't," Mackenzie said.

"I got this."

Mackenzie tapped him on top of his helmet. Chandler sat and swung his legs over the edge of the ditch. He went over, digging his fingertips into the crumbling slope to try to slow the fall. Pitch black and cooler at the bottom. The gun truck motors droned above. Chandler leaned against the slope of the ditch and listened to the engines rev then grow faint as the patrol drove away.

He wanted a cold drink. They'd been dropped off the same way the night before. The noise and light a distraction to make anyone watching think the patrol was making a quick sweep before moving on. He didn't know if the ruse would still work. Insurgents might lay in wait in the desert or inside the building, waiting until the gun trucks had gone.

Chandler shrugged into his assault pack. He cinched the shoulder straps and turned on his night vision. In the glow, Gibson tied his bootlaces and Witkowski crossed himself and Vogel aimed the over-under barrels of his weapon down the length of the ditch. He flashed the infrared knob on his goggles twice at Chandler, indicating he was ready.

Chandler licked his lips. When it was time, he wrapped his thumb and index finger around the carbine's charging handle. He pulled the rod a quarter of an inch, feeling for the tension of a loaded shell. He sank his fingers into the sand and clawed up the slope. The others followed and spread out along the top of the ditch.

Starlight shone on the desert and the building. Chandler thought about his bedroom in the house where he'd lived with Jim and Judy Eton. The foster child who'd stayed there before him had decorated the ceiling with decals of stars and planets. The room lit up when the lights were turned off. He'd lie beneath the brilliance of another boy's phony universe, imagining someplace else.

The nighttime wind swept across the desert. The sand whistled in his nostrils. Chandler swallowed and rose up from the ditch, his carbine leveled at the building. He limped a few steps then ran as fast as he could and tried to ignore the pain.

There was no ambush but the soldiers searched in and around the empty building anyway. After they'd checked for hidden bombs Chandler radioed the patrol and told them the area was clear. Upstairs, he unfolded his stool beside the second-floor window and leaned the assault pack under the ledge and angled the long antenna outside. He laid the carbine on his thighs and watched the highway through his night vision.

"Vogel's pissed," said Gibson. He reclined against the concrete wall next to the window with his knees drawn in against his ammunition pouches, scrolling through pictures on his iPod.

"Big surprise," Chandler said.

"He thought there was gonna be a firefight," said Gibson.

"Not tonight," Chandler said.

"I did, too," said Gibson. "We're sitting ducks here."

"Scared?" Chandler said.

Gibson shrugged and lit a cigarette with his Zippo. "I'm not scared," he said.

In the corner, Witkowski slept curled on his side, using his assault pack for a pillow. Vogel had stretched out beside him. His hands were folded across his chest and he looked as if he'd been laid out for a funeral.

"I can't sleep outside the wire," Chandler said.

"Vogel's awake," said Gibson. "He's listening to us."

"Think so?" Chandler said.

"I live with the guy," said Gibson. "He never sleeps. Lies perfectly still. Doesn't budge. But he's awake."

Chandler opened another pack of *Gauloise.* He tapped one out and lit it and exhaled hard. He lifted his goggles and looked at the two shapes lying on the floor in the darkness and listened to their breathing.

"I meant what I said," Gibson told him.

"I believe you," said Chandler.

"I'm not scared," Gibson said.

The wind shifted. Through the window Chandler smelled the burnt sweetness from the refinery stacks. The sedan he'd torched that morning remained on the highway, its charred frame silhouetted against the backdrop of the flat desert. He wiped his face with a cravat and pressed it over his mouth to muffle a cough. Then he swung his night vision down and lit another cigarette and cupped the burning tip between his knees, thinking.

He sat that way for a long time, trying to ignore pain in his legs and feet, the heat and the boredom. He thought about the first time he'd eaten fresh corned beef. The hamster he'd named Max that was long dead. A pretty girl visiting the lake one summer whose name he'd been too drunk to remember. An Xbox 360. About the sublet his roommate, Buggman, had signed and if his things would still be there when he got home. Sergeant Parker, the way her hips sashayed as she walked across the motor pool and why that made him smile. He thought about the G.I. Bill paperwork he'd have to fill out before returning to college in the fall and if that was a good idea. The televisions in the chow hall were still broadcasting the campus slaughter at Virginia Tech. Thinking about what that must've been like made his mouth dry up. The victims huddled beneath the desks like prey, whimpers and the ear-splitting shots, the ping of spent shell casings bouncing on the floor, footsteps closing in. How after a couple trips downrange, it'd be a terrible way for him to go. He considered using his savings to buy a chopped Colt Python or a Glock 29. Both packed oomph and could be hidden in a backpack. What it would mean if he got caught, being labeled a deranged veteran with a gun even though he figured that's what most civilians thought about him anyway. And he tried, and failed, not to think about what he always thought about when he was thinking. His tour in Afghanistan and what happened in the wheat field. That was always with him. The images and the voices like a radio or a television playing in the background. Then he thought about what Flowers had told him about the mission change and if he had enough luck to make it through another battle or accident. About dying beside strangers, sitting in the observation post or strapped inside a gun truck somewhere out in the endless ocean of burning sand.

Yup, he thought. You think too much.

Headlights from a pick-up truck approached on the highway. Chandler held his breath as the truck slowed to pass the sedan. The naked frame like an animal skeleton in the white glare of the high beams before the truck sped up and kept driving north. After it'd gone, Chandler ducked under the window and lit a new cigarette. His hands shook as he cupped them to mask the flame from his lighter.

"Hajjis?" Gibson said.

"Rubberneckers," said Chandler. "They didn't stop."

"Vogel can't get a break," Gibson said. He smiled in the dim light from his iPod.

"Pictures from home?" Chandler said.

"Strawberries," said Gibson. "I'm gonna plant some."

"In Tennessee?" Chandler said.

"Alabama," said Gibson. "Town straddles the state line. The post office, that's in Tennessee, but my house is on the Alabama side. My people don't grow anything there."

"Then where will you plant the strawberries?"

"Here in Iraq. On top of one of the Hesco barricades outside our trailer."

Chandler stamped out his cigarette and lit up another. He lifted the handset and called the gun trucks and after they responded and he knew the radio worked he clipped the handset to the top of his pack.

"Too hot for strawberries," Chandler said.

"That's what Vogel told me," said Gibson.

"Build a model or a puzzle," Chandler said.

"Seeds are already in the mail," said Gibson.

Chandler pulled back his sleeve and looked at his wristwatch. The time was 0230 and it was hot, at least one hundred and ten degrees, inside the concrete structure. He drew on his cigarette then stamped it out and glanced at the staircase behind him. After they'd cleared the building, Gibson had opened a bag of nuts and scattered them up the stone steps leading to the second floor. Now, a small desert mouse looked at the soldiers from the top of the landing. It balanced on its haunches and gnawed on one of the nuts. Chandler reached for the thermos in his assault pack. He sipped the cold coffee and watched the mouse until it crawled away.

"You've got good instincts," he said.

"Strawberries should get enough sun," Gibson said. "Lots of bottled mineral water for them to drink."

"No. The peanuts," said Chandler. "On the staircase."

"They're pistachios," Gibson said. "Big difference."

Gibson turned off his iPod and put it in his thigh pocket. He lit a cigarette then began to open and close the Zippo with his thumb. The metallic clang echoed loud off the concrete walls.

"Vogel's idea," he said. "He wanted to drop crumpled newspapers, so the Hajjis couldn't sneak up on us. Think he read about it in one of his books. I scrounged around the FOB but I didn't find any extra copies of *Stars and Stripes*. I was going to eat those pistachios for a snack."

In the corner, Witkowski mumbled in Polish before he rolled over and began to snore.

"Insurgents," Chandler said. "Someday they're gonna hit this place."

"I'm not scared," said Gibson.

"No. You're not," Chandler said.

"I'll prove it," said Gibson.

There was a loud scratching of Velcro as Gibson opened a pouch on his ammunition vest and held out what was inside. Chandler took it and in the darkness he thought it was an apple until he hefted the weight in his palm. He ran his fingers around the smooth body, feeling for the tape covering the pin and spoon before he gave it back.

"Where'd you get the hand grenade?" he said.

"Batista," said Gibson. "Keeps it in his desk in the orderly room. He doesn't need it."

"Put that thing away," Chandler said.

"Not gonna take it?" said Gibson.

"Put it away," Chandler said. "Don't let me see it again."

He pinched the corners of his eyes then rubbed the bridge of nose. Gibson watched him for a long time. He stowed the grenade in its pouch and straightened up against the wall, toying with his Zippo.

"The guys from my armory," he finally said. "Deployed to

the Sunni triangle while I was in basic training. Then they came home and I was the only one who hadn't been downrange. On drill weekend, civilians would see me in uniform and thank me for serving but I hadn't served at all. You understand."

Vogel groaned. He sat and smacked the dust on his uniform and arched his big shoulders.

"Gonna tear my ears off," he said.

"You should be nice to me," said Gibson.

"Shut up, fool," Vogel said. "Save that stupid shit for when you go back to stocking paint at the hardware store."

"I drive the forklift," said Gibson.

"Don't listen to this clown, corporal," Vogel said. "Ask him who attacked the World Trade Center. He thinks it was Saddam Hussein. Let him babble on for a few more minutes and he'll really start talking complete nonsense. Like how he was raised by a witch."

"That's a lie," said Gibson. "I drive the forklift."

"Keep the noise down," Chandler said.

"Get away from that window," Vogel said. "You know why you're here. Fucking yokel. Maybe you'll get a taste of combat before you go home. Bust a cap in some Hajji. Rednecks still gonna kick your narrow ass at the bowling alley on Saturday nights."

"I'll kill you," Gibson said.

"I wish you would," Vogel told him.

They sat in the dark and didn't move. When it was quiet again, Vogel got up, staring, as he buckled his helmet chinstrap. Gibson rose off the wall and looked at the floor. He walked to the staircase landing and sat on the top step. He aimed his carbine down the stairs, mumbling and tapping his heel.

Chandler breathed, then lowered his goggles and looked out the window at the wrecked sedan on the highway. He lit a cigarette and waited in the dark, listening to the soles of Vogel's boots squeak as he crossed the concrete floor towards him. Chandler inched his stool to one side of the window so there'd be room for both of them to sit.

CHAPTER SEVEN

VOGEL CAME TO THE window carrying his stool. It had aluminum legs and a canvas seat and was the same as Chandler's. He sat down and leaned his weapon against the wall and unwrapped a sandwich from the chow hall he'd brought in his assault pack. The thick, hot air inside the room was flushed with the smell of mustard, red onion, and sourdough. Vogel took a big bite, moaning and chewing with his muscular jaws.

"Bacon on roast beef," he said. "Motherfucker. That's delicious."

The tip of Chandler's cigarette glowed as he puffed on it. Crackle of tobacco and wheezing deep inside his chest. He coughed and spat through the open window then gently rubbed his right shin.

"Try getting laid," Vogel said. "Break one off. While you still can."

"There a clock ticking somewhere?" Chandler said.

"You know what's coming," said Vogel. "Your buddy told you."

"First sergeant's not my buddy," Chandler said.

"Whatever." Vogel finished his sandwich. He sucked his fingertips then took another sandwich from his pack and set it on the window ledge. He glanced at Gibson sitting on the stairs and Witkowski sleeping in the corner and slid his stool closer to Chandler.

"They're gonna let us fight," Vogel said.

"Maybe," said Chandler.

"It'll be the tits," Vogel said.

"I think you don't know what you're talking about," Chandler said.

"You've seen the elephant," Vogel said. "Purple Heart and a CIB. I want some of that."

"Not worth it," said Chandler.

"Compensation check," said Vogel. "Free healthcare. *Niños* go to college for free."

"That's a myth," said Chandler.

"Respect," said Vogel.

"Your kids still have to pay for college."

Vogel pecked at the crumbs in his lap. He put his boot on the window ledge and took his weapon from the wall and balanced the grenade launcher on his kneecap with the barrel pointed outside at the highway. "Fucking with me? Kids don't get free tuition?"

Chandler shook his head.

"Zepeda was a dickweed," said Vogel. "Should've never listened to his bullshit."

"Is that the guy I got sent here to replace?" Chandler said.

"That's him," said Vogel.

"Who shot him?" Chandler said.

"He shot himself," said Vogel.

"Was he depressed?" Chandler said.

"He was a fucking ding dong."

Chandler lit another cigarette and waited in the heat and darkness. Vogel sucked his teeth. Then he laughed quietly and mimed the steps for unloading a semi-automatic pistol in the dim light that shone through the window.

"Gimmick with his Beretta," said Vogel. "Sergeant Z, he's a cop back in the world, tried to show us how fast he could do it. Missed a step. Cranked a round into the blast wall at point-blank range. Bullet ricocheted into his cheek. Freaked everybody out."

Chandler rubbed the side of his face, imagining a mouthful of blood and broken teeth.

"Best part," said Vogel. "Gibson pissed himself like a little girl."

"That's not true," Gibson said from the stairway.

"Yeah he did," Vogel said. "And then Flowers doctored the report."

"Wouldn't be the first time," said Chandler. "Surprised he didn't give him a medal."

"Weapons malfunction," Vogel said. "Non-battle casualty."

Chandler nodded and stamped out his cigarette. He arched his back and looked at the road, thinking. Vogel sat beside him in the blackness. Witkowski snored in the corner. Gibson tapped his foot on the stairs. Far off in the night sky above the horizon, Chandler thought he saw the gleam of a plunging star or the wing lights of an airplane but he couldn't be sure.

"I stole your job," he finally said.

Vogel shrugged. "Mackenzie sat on my promotion paperwork too long."

"After Zepeda left," Chandler said. "This was going to be your fire team. You're senior specialist in this squad. Maybe even the platoon. You'd have plugged the vacancy. That's how it works in the National Guard, right? It's different from active duty. I'm still learning."

"Let's just say I was all jazzed up for people to start calling me Corporal or Sergeant Vogel. Then you showed up."

Chandler leaned on his elbows and wrung his hands. Then he lit another cigarette and blew the smoke out through the window and talked about Afghanistan, how it was different from Iraq. How it felt like being in a real war. Sandbags on the perimeter of their outpost and bunkers and canvas tents where they slept on musty cots inches apart. Sharing care packages so they wouldn't have to eat rehydrated field rations at chow time. Long patrols through the wheat fields and stands of trees. Color of the hills. About the dry wind and the dust that turned into a slippery sludge in the rain. How after their deployment ended, the world would be a better place and then he told Vogel about the ambush and the firefight and the way it had made him feel. How he still craved it like he now craved coffee and cigarettes and a part of him yearned to feel that sensation one more time.

He didn't talk about what'd happened after the landmine exploded or about the helicopter flight to the hospital at Bagram airfield. Lying on a stretcher next to Tran, who sobbed and yelled at the crew chief and flight medic to open the doors and push him out over the mountains, calling them cocksuckers and motherfuckers when they didn't. Staring at the body bags with Reed and Dempsey inside. Feeling ashamed because he was still alive.

When the dust-off landed, his stretcher was unloaded onto a cart and he was wheeled into the hospital. The lights on the triage room ceiling so bright he thought he would burn. He was sick and tried to vomit but couldn't. They were women, the medics and doctors and nurses, and they sliced off his fatigues and boots and bandages stiff with dried blood until he lay naked on the stretcher, his crotch covered by a paper towel, squinting under the lights. Everything smelled clean. Fingertips sheathed in latex against his skin. Hoses plugged into the veins in his arms and his chest shaved and nodes glued to the bare patches and then giggling as a finger was inserted into his rectum. The pang of what sounded like marbles splashing into a steel pan and when he looked saw the tweezers and thin probe separating the gnarled hunks of metal and rock from the shreds of gore. The medic who sat beside him wore a mask and blinked with blueberry eyes and whispered in a Philadelphia twang not to worry about what he saw. Most of the torn flesh inside him belonged to someone else and soon it'd be gone, she said. The surgeons were ready. He was tired and he was very afraid. Afraid of the metallic taste of anesthesia creeping through the mask strapped over his mouth. The sleep he couldn't fight. Afraid that he'd wake up and not have legs anymore.

Vogel raised his goggles over his helmet. He leaned forward and peered through the open window, as if he'd seen something out among the sand and scrub grass, behind the shadow of the wrecked sedan far off on the highway. He unbuckled his chinstrap and took off his helmet. Then he scratched his head and smoothed his hair flat and wiped his forehead dry with a sleeve. He put his helmet on and reached for the sandwich but pulled his hand back. He left the sandwich on the window ledge in its plastic wrapping.

"It was an accident?" Vogel said. "You were walking to the chopper then boom?"

"An old Soviet landmine," said Chandler. "Taliban had nothing to do with it."

"I figured you'd done something hardcore, like maybe took out a bunker or something," Vogel said.

Chandler shook his head. "I was never brave. That was all Flowers. Guy acts like he did me a favor."

"And the Vietnamese guy?" Vogel said.

"Tran quit," Chandler said. "Went into a coma at Landstuhl then his body turned itself off. Told me he didn't want to go on. And after I'd saw where he got hit, down there, I really couldn't blame him so I stopped trying to stop him."

He told Vogel how he was flown stateside and assigned to a rear-detachment company, that's where he'd taken up smoking, until his legs were no longer swollen and purple from the infection. How after he didn't need crutches to walk he was given a job working at the brigade gymnasium and then promoted to corporal six months before his enlistment ended.

"Whoever had keys to the gym had to be a non-commissioned officer," he said. "I was leaving the regular army. My supervisors didn't think I'd ever get called up from the reserves."

"This is all so fucking stupid," Vogel said.

Chandler raised his night-vision goggles. He flicked his cigarette. The burning tip tumbled through the darkness and exploded in a shower of orange sparks when it smacked against the far wall.

"Screw you," he said. "I was done. I got into college, a good one.

Then I got drafted and sent to this armpit because some goofball shot himself in the face."

"Touché," Vogel said.

They sat in the dark for a long time and listened to the nighttime wind out in the desert.

"Still hope they let us fight," Vogel said.

"Of course you do," said Chandler.

"This is humiliating," Vogel said. "I'd rather live by the minute than die by the day."

Chandler shrugged. He turned and looked at Gibson and Witkowski. "Who else knows?"

"They all do," said Vogel. "Gonna be a mission change soon. But nobody knows what."

"You didn't find out from Flowers?" Chandler said.

Vogel shook his head. "Batista. Has a hard on for Iraq. Wishes we'd get extended three months."

"Man with a plan," Chandler said.

"Stupid plan," Vogel said. "Shorty's one of those migrant Mexicans who doesn't give a fuck about a green card. He's trying to bankroll the cash for a down payment on a piece of shit apartment building. Wants to play slumlord. Rent to illegals from his piss-pot town south of the border. Calls it his masterstroke. Dumb fucker doesn't even know what that means. He's asked me five times where I'm from in Mexico. My mother's parents came from there. And when I tell Shorty I'm from Little Village, born and bred on the south side of Chicago, guy looks at me and blinks."

Chandler lowered his night vision. He turned the optic and adjusted the focus until he could see the wreckage of the sedan. "You got a better idea?"

"I'll come up with something," said Vogel.

"Hard to decide," Chandler said. "Since you got back from leave. I know what it's like."

"Not gonna talk about it," said Vogel.

"Realized your friends really weren't your friends anymore,"

Chandler said.

"Keep digging," said Vogel.

"And the things you liked to do weren't as much fun," Chandler said.

"You don't know shit," said Vogel.

"No. I don't know anything," Chandler said.

"Heard the rumors?" said Vogel.

"I'm a replacement," Chandler said. "Nobody tells me anything."

"I robbed a bodega," said Vogel. "Strangled a hooker. My favorite's the one about how I blew twenty-five grand at a strip club. Bought every last bottle of top-shelf booze, paid for the private VIP room and then poured out all the liquor on a stripper's boobies. Didn't drink a drop."

"That's a good rumor," Chandler said.

"Goddamn right it is," said Vogel.

Chandler lit a cigarette. "I wanna go home," he said. "Don't always know why. Just do."

"You're just scared you'll get wounded again," said Vogel.

"Think I'm going to be killed," Chandler said. "But that's not what I'm afraid of."

They sat quietly for a long time. Vogel nudged the sandwich across the window ledge until it was in front of Chandler then he swung his night vision down over his eyes and stared at the highway. "Hungry?"

"I could eat," Chandler said.

"Need some water?" said Vogel.

"I need some advice," Chandler said.

"About what?" Vogel said.

"Getting laid."

Vogel snorted and clucked his tongue. "That," he said. "Start with the ginger who works in the mailroom. She sells condoms for three hundred. Aid station's got that Romanian lieutenant who's as sharp as a wrecking ball but be careful because she'll lick your butthole. And there's always the Widow Maker company. Wait until those girls escort another convoy back to the FOB. Pussy explosion."

Chandler cupped his cigarette in his palms. He took a long draw then stamped it out under the heel of his boot. "What about that sergeant. The girl who runs the commo shop?"

"Parker?" Vogel said. "Gibson wasn't kidding. Foxy bitch got an ass like a Dutch oven. I'd work her over."

"Haven't hit that yet?" Chandler said.

"Hell no," said Vogel.

"What's she got?" Chandler said.

"Got the crazy," said Vogel. "Can't pin it down. Something about her just ain't right."

Chandler pulled back his sleeve and pushed the button on his watch and saw the time was 0413. He took the sandwich from the window ledge. He unwrapped it from the plastic and held the bread to his nose and sniffed before he took a bite. He closed his eyes and chewed. The kid's absolutely right, he thought. Delicious.

CHAPTER EIGHT

THE SUN HAD RISEN and they were still watching from the window. Dirt-splattered Iraqi cars and trucks lumbered on the highway, belching black exhaust as their drivers accelerated to pass the wreckage of the sedan.

"Any water left?" Vogel said.

"Two bottles in my pack," Chandler told him. He'd removed the night-vision goggles from his helmet at dawn. He stowed them in the dump pouch on his ammunition vest then he swapped out the batteries in the radio. As the darkness ebbed, the desert was shaded a lead hue, until the sun tore a ray of fire across the sky, revealing the patches of scrub grass and the unexploded shells that bloomed out of the sand between the building and the highway.

"Not thirsty?" Vogel said.

"Take it. The water's not for me," said Chandler. He exhaled smoke out the window then spat and crushed the cigarette under the heel of his boot.

Vogel leaned his carbine with the grenade launcher against the wall. He folded his stool and buckled it to the outside of his assault pack. He stretched. Clawing at the ceiling with spread fingers then wrinkled his face and dropped to the floor, balancing on his hands.

His ammunition pouches slapped the concrete as he did push-ups. After fifty, he stood and swung his arms in a circle then squatted in the shade beside the window. He laid his weapon on his thighs and began to whisk sand off the ejection port with a small paintbrush. Sweat beaded beneath his earlobe. "What a goat fuck," he said.

"Nervous?" Chandler said.

"Cool as the other side of the pillow," Vogel said. He shut his eyes and banged the back of his helmet against the wall. He licked his lips then went back to cleaning.

Chandler inched his stool closer to the edge of the window so only half his face showed through the opening. He peeked at the highway with one eye and when no vehicles were in sight took off his helmet and scratched his face where the chinstrap had been cinched tight. He cradled his helmet. He was tired and felt his eyes close and blinked and looked up when his chin touched the ceramic chest plate in his body armor. He breathed deeply until the blood flowed then rolled his neck and put his helmet on and buckled the chinstrap again.

He lit another cigarette. The sun shone through the windows. The shadows inside grew narrow and soon they were absorbed by the light and heat. The building was about the size of the Eton's grocery but larger inside because of the second floor. Empty except for the staircase at one end. Its construction halted before the doors and windows were framed. The smooth walls and high ceiling loomed massive in the daytime.

Witkowski was still asleep in the corner. The bright sunlight crept towards him and after it shone on his face for a long time he sat up, as if an alarm had sounded. He was much older than the others but only in age and it showed in the eyes that opened suddenly and darted around the second floor of the building. "*Kurwa*," he said.

"Everything's fine," Chandler said.

Witkowski looked. Then he reached across his body and drew the pistol from the holster on his belt. Both hands clasped the handgrip. He held the pistol tight to his sternum. "It's daytime," he said.

"You're not awake," said Chandler.

Witkowski thumbed the safety catch.

"*Zatrzymać, Waclaw*," Vogel said.

Witkowski blinked then pursed his lips and exhaled. He

holstered the pistol then wiped his palm across his face. Dirt from the glove stained his ruddy cheeks.

"What happened?" he said.

They told him they didn't know. Mackenzie had radioed two hours earlier. There'd be no pick up. Hold their position and wait for orders. Back at Camp Tucson, everyone was on alert. There'd been an incident.

"Another rocket attack?" Witkowski said.

"We'd have heard that," said Vogel.

"Someone might've lost their weapon," Gibson said from the stairs.

Chandler shook his head. "If that's all that happened then they'd have come and gotten us by now."

"Where'd the gun trucks go?" Witkowski said.

Gibson stood and went to the backside of the building. The knickknacks in his pockets jingled like a janitor's keyset as he walked in a crouch. He peered into the desert then joined the others.

"The squad's about three clicks away," he said. "I see their antennas poking up from the other end of that ditch we hid in last night. They're chasing shade."

"Why are you whispering?" Vogel said.

"I don't know," said Gibson.

Witkowski pulled off his protective glasses. He had a bottle of water in his cargo pocket and he opened it and splashed his cheeks. There was a tan dirt splotch on his nose after he wiped his face again. He drank and after he'd drained the bottle spat on the floor, watching the spray of droplets fade then vanish in the sunlight.

Chandler watched him. So did Vogel, stabbing the paintbrush at the flash suppressor on the barrel of his carbine. Vogel finished his cleaning and stuffed the brush in a thigh pocket and stretched out his legs, smiling.

•

The sun rose higher. The shadows were chased out of the building and then it was so hot it hurt to breathe. Gibson lay by the wall and scrolled through pictures on his iPod. Witkowski hunched over the magnetic chess set he carried in his assault pack. Across the board, Vogel read a paperback, waiting until it was his turn.

Chandler stood and leaned against the concrete wall. He thought about how old Gibson and Witkowski were, but he didn't want to ask because he wanted his men to think he knew them and that he knew what he was doing. Chandler held the radio handset to his ear. The room was quiet except for a fart and the ticking of the pieces maneuvering on the chessboard. Sweat from under his helmet ran off his temples and nose. Cascaded down his chest and stomach and pooled at his beltline. When the highway was clear he leaned out the window. The breeze burned his face. Finally, he took off his Nomex gloves and rolled his sleeves above his forearms.

"I'm ready to go home," said Gibson.

"Five more weeks," Chandler said.

"FOB home," said Gibson. He jammed the iPod in his pocket. "Battery's dead."

Vogel grunted. He turned a page in his book with his thumb while the other hand slid his remaining rook to the center of the chessboard. "You're off your game," he said.

"Where'd you learn the language?" Witkowski said.

"Few Polskis left in the old neighborhood," said Vogel.

"Your pronunciation's old, formal."

"Good enough to get my ass kicked."

Witkowski nodded and crossed his legs. He leaned in and studied the board then sacrificed his queen. "From now on I'll talk shit about you in English," he said.

After that no one talked and soon it became too hot to enjoy smoking but Chandler lit another cigarette anyway.

Mackenzie radioed at noon. He told Chandler to pack up all their equipment and make sure there was no trace they'd been there then leave and walk across the desert to the ditch, where the patrol was hiding.

"It'd be no trouble to drive over here and get us," Witkowski said.

"Welcome to the infantry," said Chandler.

"I didn't expect the Roman legions," Witkowski said. "It's probably a hundred and twenty degrees out here. We'll melt. A man my age has options. I should've banged the new waitress at Pat's Diner. Bought a motorcycle and hauled ass down Brunswick Avenue. Instead, I had to join the Guard and volunteer for Iraq. Fuck me in the face."

They packed up the stools and books and chess pieces. The empty plastic bottles and the ones sloshing with dark urine. The cigarette butts and sandwich crumbs from the floor. Chandler collapsed the radio antenna and shouldered his assault pack. He swallowed a Motrin and waited for the soldiers to insert the dark lenses in their protective glasses and looked around the room one more time.

"Going down," Gibson said. "Getting the pistachios."

He knelt on the staircase and began to scoop up the shells. He sang "Big Rock Candy Mountain" in a nasal drawl.

Vogel smiled at Chandler. "It's like his favorite song."

They listened and waited but then the singing voice trailed off and it was quiet. Chandler turned to Vogel and Vogel turned to Witkowski.

Witkowski shook his head. "No. He knows every word by heart."

Chandler jerked his chin and the others lined up behind him and they walked to the stairs.

He called out then waited and listened. Finally, he raised his carbine and braced the stock against his shoulder. Tip of his finger light against the side of the trigger. Thumb on the selector switch. He pressed himself against the wall and stepped down.

Gibson stood between the bottom step and the doorway. His hands were cupped in a bowl topped with green pistachio shells.

His face had paled and he stared at the opposite end of the empty room.

"The heck you doing?" Chandler said.

"We almost ran down here spraying," said Vogel.

"There," Gibson said. He gestured at the corner wall. Pistachios fell through his fingers. He winced as the shells bounced at his feet. Across the room, the concrete slab was chipped and peppered with thumb-sized holes. Linear tracks of automatic-rifle fire. Reddish-brown smears streaked down the wall like veins of a river delta. The faded stains merged into a large puddle on the floor.

"That is a fuckload of blood," Vogel said.

Chandler lowered his carbine. He stepped off the stairs and crossed the room. He breathed shallowly as he neared the corner wall. He reached the edge of the stain and then stopped. The air in the room was cold. He thought about that and took another step. He stopped and couldn't move any further. As if a pair of outstretched palms pushed back against his chest. The dead told him *no* and shoved harder. He couldn't move, and now he didn't want to. He stood at the rim of the dried puddle and tapped it with his toe.

He turned and walked to the doorway. He stood in the threshold and looked at the desert, thinking. Then he took off his assault pack and set it on the floor and extended the long antenna. He radioed Mackenzie and told him what they'd found.

"Good. Now we don't have to walk," said Witkowski.

Chandler slung his carbine and lit a cigarette. He was thirsty and his hands shook. He put them in his pockets and squeezed the whistle until they stopped. He drew hard on the cigarette and leaned against the doorway, bombarded by flies as he lifted his face to the hot afternoon sun.

CHAPTER NINE

THE INTERPRETER WAS AN Iraqi. A man in his early 60s they called "Sundance," but that wasn't his name. He squatted on his heels, studying the bullet holes in the wall and the faded bloodstain on the floor.

"Wicked men," he said. "They ruined everything."

He stood and wrapped his leathered face with a red-and-white checkered *shemagh* and walked to the door. His black eyes glanced at Chandler leaning against the wall, drinking a can of orange soda from Mackenzie's gun truck. Then he went outside to where the vehicles had parked.

"The matter with him?" said Lazlo, the sergeant whose truck Chandler had ridden in the day before.

Mackenzie sat on the concrete staircase. Chin cradled in his palm. The Kool between his fingertips had burned to the filter, stone-colored ash hanging in a crescent. His eye twitched. He stared for a long time, as if looking through a window to someplace else.

"Sectarian payback," Mackenzie finally said. "Genocide's a better word. In Najaf, the bodies would've been left behind as a warning. Someone took these departed little darlings back home."

Lazlo scraped under his thumbnail with the tip of the AK-47 bayonet.

"Hajji," he said. "Snatched three of our guys up north last month. Those animals cut off the heads. And their dicks. Dumped the guys in a shit-filled canal. Fucking media ate that up."

Mackenzie dropped the cigarette butt. Ash shattered on the

stairs. His eye twitched as he put his protective glasses on. He turned and looked up at Lazlo through dark lenses coated with dust.

"You don't get out of the truck," he said.

"And I won't do it again," Lazlo told him. He left and walked to his gun truck. On the roof, the driver and gunner straddled the light machine gun mounted in the turret. The soldiers laughed in the sunshine. Lazlo yelled at them over the noise of the idling engines then climbed into the front seat and slammed the armored door.

Chandler watched and listened. He'd spoken only a few words since the patrol had arrived at the listening post. His legs were sore and he was tired and hungry. He fingered the whistle in his front pocket, thinking about the ambush in Afghanistan. Flowers standing over the insurgent shot dead in the ditchwater. Swoosh of the war club and feathers swinging through the air perfumed in cordite. The dull pop when the skull smashed open. Chandler had never agreed with that. But now he thought he understood why.

"What'd the first sergeant say?" Chandler said.

"Take pictures," said Mackenzie. "Enough for a statement. I'll write it up this time."

"We'd no idea this was here," Chandler said.

Mackenzie shook his head. "You couldn't. Not in the dark. Not with night vision."

He patted the pockets on his pants and sleeves. Chandler crossed the room holding a pack of cigarettes. He flipped two though the opening. Mackenzie lit one and blew the smoke out his nose, holding the smoldering tip upright like a flaming match.

"How many a day?" he said.

"Four. Sometimes five packs," Chandler said.

"God," said Mackenzie.

"Sergeant. We should've gone back by now," Chandler said.

A soldier was raped on Camp Tucson. It'd happened near the showers. He showed up at the aid station and told the medics he'd been drugged unconscious then sodomized. The camp was locked down. Trailers were being searched. The patrol remained outside the wire in case the attacker tried to escape.

"Escape to where?" Chandler said.

"Ask the big brains in operations," said Mackenzie.

"They don't need us out here," Chandler said.

Mackenzie dropped the cigarette on the steps and ground it out with his boot. He jerked his head at the bullet holes in the wall and bloodstain on the floor. "They do now."

Witkowski took pictures of the wall and the floor. Then he switched settings on the camera and retraced his steps and began to shoot video.

"No," he said. "Witkowski's Best Polish Cleaning doesn't service crimes or accidents."

"Too gross?" said Vogel, who trailed and directed where to zoom in or pan out for effect.

"Expensive," Witkowski said. "You need a special license. Biohazard suits. I've never cleaned up anything like this before."

Gibson sat by the opposite wall where they'd leaned their assault packs. He'd collected the pistachios off the stairs and ate them slowly, piling the shells on the cracked and dusty floor.

"My uncle and me once skinned a doe in his garage," he said.

"Shut up," said Vogel.

Chandler watched and listened. After a long time he stepped outside. The building still felt cold and that made him ill. He lit a cigarette and looked beyond the parked gun trucks across the open desert. A battle was fought here in the early hours of the invasion. The sun shone bright, and through the heat vapors the oil refinery stacks and the watchtowers and berm loomed around Camp Tucson. Trash from the highway blew across the flat plain dotted with pieces of airburst artillery shrapnel, jagged hunks shaped like lawnmower blades. Tail fins of undetonated sixty-millimeter mortar shells canted in the sand like the markers in a derelict graveyard.

In a day or two, Golf Company would receive a new mission,

Chandler thought. Not knowing the details wrung his insides like a dishtowel. He weighed the many possibilities: Guards at the detention center at Camp Joplin. Sentries on the combat outposts and checkpoints around Anbar Province. Kicking in doors running foot patrols along Haifa Street or in Sadr City. He smoked, thinking about himself and his men. Again, about how they'd all hold up in a firefight. If they'd watch his back or if it'd be every man for himself.

When he returned inside, the soldiers farted and laughed and took turns with the camera, posing for portraits. Gibson crawled on his hands and knees and lapped at the faded blood on the floor. Witkowski grabbed his crotch and flashed his middle finger. Vogel roared like a grizzly and aimed his weapon and pretended to shoot at the bullet holes in the wall.

"Haunted house," Vogel said. "Every neighborhood's got one."

"Hajji believes in ghosts?" Gibson said.

"Believes the same shit we do," said Vogel.

Witkowski winked at Chandler. "The young man has a theory about what happened here. You'll like it."

Vogel slung his weapon. He raised his arms high, like a revival preacher preparing to launch into a sermon before grabbing a poisonous snake. He stalked across the room and pressed his palms and the side of his face against the wall and smiled and closed his eyes.

"They were Sunnis," Vogel said. "Lined up here. But they got fucking scared shitless and huddled in the corner, like you know they do, rocking back and forth, finger fucking those prayer beads they always carry. The others were Mehdi Army. Or Iraqi police. Same thing. They waited for the signal."

He backed to the center of the room and held the twin pistol grips of an imaginary tommy gun that he shook and raked back and forth along the length of the wall then down onto the floor.

"*Bah, dah, bah, dah, bah, dah, bah, dah, bah, dah, bah, dah, bah, dah, bah, dah, bah, dah, bah, dah, bah, dah, bah, dah, bah, dah, bah, dah, bah, dah, bah.*"

They all looked at the bullet holes and the blood on the floor. Quiet for a long time until Witkowski shivered and sucked in his breath. "Feel that?" he said.

"Spooky," Gibson said.

"Like I told you, a haunted house," said Vogel. "And aren't we a bunch of suckers. Hajji was never gonna attack us in here. He thinks this place is bad news."

They shouldered their packs and weapons and left.

Outside in the heat and sun, Mackenzie sat in the front seat of his gun truck. He pressed a radio handset to his ear, dangling his legs out of the open hatch.

Chandler laid his assault pack atop the hood of the vehicle and gave him the memory card from Witkowski's camera. "There's personal photos on there," Chandler said.

"Tough," said Mackenzie. "After S-2 makes their copies, I'm gonna scrub it clean."

"He won't like that," Chandler said.

"Won't like the stockade, either," said Mackenzie. "One of his dumb buddies will post it on *LiveLeak*. Yes, they will. We'll all end up in a cell next to those assholes from Abu Ghraib."

Chandler thought about that, then nodded. He lit up and exhaled at his reflection staring back in the dirty windshield.

"I'm not going back in that building," he said. "Someone else can take a turn."

"Won't have to," Mackenzie said. "Your buddy called."

"Can we leave now?"

"Sure can," Mackenzie said. "And we're gonna be off duty until tomorrow morning."

He told Chandler to eat breakfast then gather his team for maintenance on the vehicles and radios and weapons. Load their gun truck with ammunition and fuel and water. And pack their rucksacks and duffle bags.

"Are we taking a trip?" Chandler said.

Mackenzie shrugged. "Rumor is our replacements showed up

early. That we gotta get ready to sign over all our gear. That fool Lazlo thinks he's gonna be home in time for Father's Day."

"That's not happening," Chandler said.

"Oh no," said Mackenzie. "Fully expect we'll get boned in the ass. I'm even thinking about changing our squad's call sign. Something real Hollywood."

"What's that?" Chandler said.

"Woolly Bugger," said Mackenzie. He spat and thumbed at the empty seat behind him.

CHAPTER TEN

THE PATROL DROVE AWAY from the listening post, speeding across the desert in the bright afternoon sun. They entered the camp and unloaded weapons at the clearing barrels then refueled the gun trucks and parked in the motor pool.

Chandler got out of Mackenzie's vehicle. He stretched out his legs one at a time and flexed his ankles. He watched the soldiers lock up and gather their equipment for the long hike up to the main section of camp and the trailers where they lived.

"Taking your creepy pictures to S-2," Mackenzie said.

"I'm going to the orderly room," said Chandler.

"Have fun," Mackenzie said. He removed his protective glasses and squinted at the sun.

Chandler lit a cigarette and shouldered his assault pack. He tried to ignore the pain in his shins. "Don't you want to know?" he said.

"Already got a good idea," Mackenzie said. His left eye twitched.

"This mission change. Is it gonna put us in a jam?"

"Not saying shit," Mackenzie said. "Not until the commander does. Let him be the bearer of bad news. What he gets paid for."

"I'm gonna come right out and ask," said Chandler.

"Won't make any difference," Mackenzie said.

"Might make all the difference," said Chandler.

"No. Not to me," Mackenzie said. "I don't mind being kept in the dark like a mushroom."

Chandler snuffed out his cigarette and stashed the butt in his pocket. He needed sleep and felt himself losing his patience. "I'm going to the orderly room."

"Check the mail," Mackenzie said. "And say hi to your buddy for me."

Mackenzie buckled his carbine and helmet to his assault pack and headed to the trailers. The heels of his boots dragged on the soft sand and left a trail of shallow skid marks in his wake.

Gibson sat nearby in front of the row of parked gun trucks and picked his acne. Witkowski staggered in circles. They looked delirious with exhaustion, sweaty and dirty. Vogel began to knock out pushups in the burning sand.

"Want us to stay?" he said. His cheeks turned purple as he pumped.

Chandler waved off a fly and shook his head.

"Go do whatever mushrooms do."

He crossed the motor pool and mounted the walkway between the shacks. He opened the orderly room door and stepped into the artificial cold. Flowers sat behind his desk. Steam curled from a Styrofoam cup of noodles he stirred with one of his chopsticks. Ice shards spat from the air conditioner.

In the center of the room, Batista hopped across the floorboards. Dust shook off the walls and furniture. The trash pail beside his desk was filled with empty energy drink cans. He grunted and snatched the air and jammed his fists hard against his hips, imitating a doggy-style thrust.

"I'm the Ether Bunny," he said. "Coming to get you, corporal. Coming to get you."

Chandler backed the door shut and leveled his carbine at Batista's chest.

"Stop," Flowers said. "Shorty drank a 12-pack of those green Monsters. You're not the only one who's been up all night."

"Homeboy in finance got ass raped," Batista said.

Chandler lowered his carbine and let it hang from the sling.

"Which one?" he said.

"Skinny E-3 with the Ukrainian accent and funny teeth," Flowers told him.

"Got his asshole all busted out," said Batista.

Chandler tried to remember the face but couldn't. He patted Batista on the shoulder as he stepped past and removed the radio and the extra batteries from his assault pack. He plugged the batteries into the charger and eyed the packages and letters stacked on the floor.

He saw a package in the pile addressed to him. The handwriting was Judy Eton's. Chandler took it and sat in a folding chair. He spun the package and listened to the tumble within, then held it up and read the list of contents written on the label.

"Think it over?" Flowers said.

"Think what over?" Chandler said.

"That thing we talked about," Flowers said. "You've had plenty of time to weigh all the angles."

"That," said Chandler. "I thought about it."

Flowers pecked at the cup of noodles. He looked over the rim of the cup at Chandler and the red thumbtacks in the map on the wall. "I need to know now. If you've changed your mind," he said.

"Embrace your inner Fobbit, corporal," said Batista.

Chandler listened to the static hiss from the radio, thinking.

"I think I think too much," he finally said.

"Then why the fuck are you bothering me?" said Flowers. He slurped down the last of the noodles and set the cup beside the war club on the edge of his desk. The air conditioner coughed a chip of ice onto his forearm. He brushed it to the floor then began to wipe his chopsticks with a handkerchief.

"Wanted to get the mail," Chandler said. He spun the package again then set it in his lap.

"Nothing you wanted to ask about?" Flowers said.

"Now it doesn't seem important."

"Ask anyway," Flowers said. He looked across the desk at

Chandler with his narrow eyes and waited.

"First sergeant. Is there mail?" Chandler said.

Flowers shrugged. "Obviously. What's in the box, wise ass?"

"Beef jerky, Pringles, instant coffee, toothpaste, and socks," Chandler said.

"You don't eat Pringles," Flowers said.

"It's from my mother," Chandler said.

"No. It's not," said Flowers.

"You know what I meant," Chandler said.

Flowers smiled. "The cross breed," he said. "Your man Vogel. He also got a package. It's from some clown named John Smith."

"I'll make sure he gets it," Chandler said.

"I sense contraband," said Flowers.

"Like what?"

"Shampoo bottles filled with Absolut and Patrón."

Chandler tightened his grip on the package in his lap. "Want me to track him down?"

"Go," said Flowers. "Second squad, second platoon has a formation at 1600 tomorrow, after maintenance. Captain Ingram will have an answer to the question that you didn't come in here to ask."

They walked across the motor pool and onto the trail that led to the main swath of camp. Vogel laced his fingers together like a basket to brace his care package against his body armor.

"Told you not to wait," Chandler said.

"Too risky," said Vogel. "Didn't want to get pulled out of the gym to walk back down here and write another statement."

"Top thinks you've got contraband," Chandler said.

"So what?" Vogel said. "Don't give two shits what that loony dickhead thinks. Can't stop the boys on the block if they want to represent for the three-one-two and hook up the troops."

"You get caught," Chandler said. "First sergeant's going to hook me up."

"Roger that," Vogel said.

Witkowski hefted the automatic rifle onto his shoulder. "But no envelope for me?" he said.

"I looked," said Chandler.

"It'd be large and brown," Witkowski said.

"We'll check again tomorrow," Chandler said. "After we take care of our business."

He told the soldiers about the formation scheduled for the next day. In the morning after breakfast, Gibson would sign out the keys to the gun truck then drive it to the maintenance bay. Vogel would clean and test fire the heavy machinegun, and draw ammunition, smoke grenades and signal flares. Witkowski would replace the saline packs in the first-aid kit, rinse the ice chest, make sure they had traffic cones and spike strips and MREs and body bags. Chandler told them he'd inspect everything before they joined the rest of the squad.

"Never touched half of what we were issued," Witkowski said.

"That's why I'm gonna check it over," Chandler said.

"Lot to get done in one day," Gibson said.

Chandler nodded. "Pretend your life depends on it."

They split up at the intersection of the trail, a spot where the packed dirt turned into a pathway paved with large gravel stones. The three soldiers mounted a raised walkway between the rows of trailers and turned out of sight at the end of the block.

Chandler thought about what their new mission might be and the package under his arm. He was out of energy and stumbled as he walked along the gravel path. His ankles rolled and through the rubber treads of his boots he felt the large stones grind into the balls of his feet. The path and the wooden walkways dividing the neighborhood of trailers were deserted. Quiet except for the groan of generators that powered the lights and air conditioning. The heat of the afternoon was too much. Even for the Smurfs, Iraqi day workers who wore dark blue jumpsuits while they burned trash and washed out the port-a-johns.

He walked. Past the numbered blast barricades stacked at the entrance to each walkway. Finally, he weaved between a pair of dirt-filled barriers, onto a set of wooden planks stretching along the block where he stayed. Shrapnel fragments inside his shins scraped against the tendons. His legs sore and stiff. His right foot dragged as he negotiated the long boulevard of sand-coated boards.

"Be nice if someone sent me a box," said a voice atop one of the trailers.

It was Second Lieutenant Steven Hurd. He sat in a canvas beach chair near the edge of the flat roof. Sunbathing in his running shorts and a University of Maryland ball cap. Under the frayed and sweat-stained bill, a pair of aviator glasses shielded his eyes from the sun.

Chandler shifted the package and saluted. "Been awhile, sir. Figured you went on leave."

Hurd removed his sunglasses and leaned forward. The identification tags dangling from a chain around his neck clinked like wind chimes. Sweat on the mat of curly hairs on his back and chest, his shoulders and the strand of barbed wire and crossed rifles tattooed on his bicep.

"Deployment's easy money," Hurd said. "Not going to waste it on R&R. Got me working midnights to noon at operations with the other platoon leaders. Making PowerPoint slides for the battle captain."

Chandler set the package on the walkway. He lit a cigarette and blinked in the bright sun.

"No guts, no glory," he said.

Hurd snorted and reached under the chair for a bottle of water. Chandler watched as he drank and felt ill.

"I read your report," he said. "About the Hajjis who blew themselves up on the highway."

"Does brigade want me to rewrite it?" Chandler said.

Hurd spat between the trailers. He shook his head. "Succinct. Like an English paper."

"Thank you, sir," Chandler said.

"You go to Michigan, right?" Hurd said.

"State," Chandler said.

Hurd nodded. "Spartans. OK. What'd you study?"

"Underwater basket weaving."

They looked at each other and didn't talk. "Football or basketball?" Hurd finally said.

"Hockey," said Chandler. "I like the NHL."

"Red Wings?" Hurd said.

Chandler shook his head. "Bruins. I dig their center. Bergeron."

"Like his game?" Hurd said.

"I like that he plays even when he's hurt."

Hurd took another drink of water and held out the bottle.

Chandler shook his head. "That stuff will kill you."

Hurd set the bottle under his chair. "You don't like officers. I detect a hint of disdain in your voice."

"Sir. I don't know anything about you," Chandler said.

"I don't like officers, either," Hurd said. "Especially our company commander."

"After tomorrow," Chandler said. "Captain Ingram's not gonna have any friends."

Hurd turned up his palms then slapped them on his kneecaps. "What we signed up for," he said.

"Not me," Chandler said. "I was mostly fine with staying on the camp, working the towers and the gate, even if I did have to babysit Lazlo."

Hurd cocked his head and looked down from atop the trailer. He looked for a long time.

"What's it like to be wounded?" he finally said. "That's a dick thing to say, but I'm interested and can't think of a better way to ask."

Chandler now knew that from beneath the visor of his hat the lieutenant had been staring at the 82nd Airborne patch on his right sleeve pocket. He blinked and toyed with his cigarette.

He thought about how it'd happened so fast and wasn't too bad until the pain set in. About hobbling through the airport on convalescent leave. News of the war broadcast on the televisions. Travelers on business or vacation staring or not staring at the bandages on his legs spotted with blood. Setting off the alarms at the security checkpoint and having to explain about the metal fragments still inside him and how that'd made him feel as if he'd been defeated.

"It's not like anything at all," Chandler said. He drew on the cigarette and looked at his shadow stretching along the walkway. His stomach was sour and he was hot and sore and wanted to be someplace else. "I could tell you all the details, but if I did, and you're like most people, you'd wish I hadn't so I won't. If that's OK, sir."

"Biology," Hurd told him. "I have a degree in the field so it's my nature to be curious. I've also asked myself if I could do a second deployment if I ever got hit. Don't mean to sound like an ass."

"Wanted to be a scientist when you grew up?" Chandler said.

"I wanted to be important." Hurd put on his sunglasses and leaned back in the chair and turned his face to the sun.

Inside his trailer it was dark and cool and smelled of Freon from the air conditioner and a hint of mold. Chandler switched on the overhead bulb and waited until his eyes had adjusted to the flickering light. He set the package on the poncho liner covering his bunk.

He draped his helmet, body armor and ammunition vest over the scarecrow in the corner. The scarecrow was made from two boards nailed together in a cross. There when he moved in. He'd considered throwing it out. Sometimes he'd wake in the dark screaming at the scarecrow because in his half-sleep he would think he'd died in the wheat field in Afghanistan. That everything that'd happened since then wasn't real because he'd gone to hell. The air conditioning was set on high and Chandler shivered in his sweat-soaked T-shirt.

He sat on his bunk and opened the top drawer. He reached in his pocket and took out the whistle that was supposed to have been a farewell present for Sergeant Reed.

Chandler studied the streaks of mud he'd never washed off. After a long time, he raised the whistle to his lips and blew softly. The little pea inside rattled and moaned. He held the whistle a while longer, thinking, then put it in the drawer and closed it and began to undress.

By the time he'd walked back from the showers, his mouth was dry and his stomach tight. Chandler went inside and locked the trailer door. He slipped off his sneakers then sat on the edge of his bunk in his running shorts. He leaned forward and traced his fingertips along his calves and shins, feeling for any new shrapnel fragments protruding from the cracked, hairless skin. Most of the pieces were tiny, like grains of sand. He'd personally removed more than one hundred pieces since he was wounded, but he never kept them.

When he was finished, he picked up the package from Judy Eton. He shook it once, then reached in the nightstand for his switchblade and snapped it open and slashed the tape sealing the lid.

Chandler emptied the box. He set the packets of instant coffee aside. Threw the beef jerky and bubble wrap in the trash. He opened the Pringles and looked for a can of beer hidden inside and when he saw there wasn't one he tossed that in the trash, too. At the bottom of the box, a long envelope and six pairs of white tube socks, each rolled to the size of a fist.

Chandler unrolled the socks. Cached inside were little airplane bottles of Maker's Mark, Jack Daniels and Wild Turkey. He lined the bottles on the nightstand. He opened one without looking at the label and poured it into his canteen cup. He held the steel rim under his nostrils and sniffed until they burned and then he drank the bourbon down fast. His body shook.

He opened the envelope with his switchblade and unfolded

the letter. It was two pages long, written in Judy's tight cursive. He read it. Then he reread the part about how the cancer had shriveled Jim Eton down to an empty husk, and the old man died the same day he was supposed to be sent home from the hospital.

Chandler set the letter beside him on his bunk. His hands shook. He sniffed and bit his lip until his eyes stopped watering then leaned forward, massaging his forehead. He began to say, "I love you, pop," but even though he could feel the words inside his head his lips did not move. He breathed deep, thinking about the things he'd been through so far in life and about what he feared would happen soon. Chandler took another bottle from the nightstand. He unscrewed the cap and poured another shot into his canteen cup.

The gun truck was spotted with beads of water. Little pools that shimmered then shrank in the sunshine. Chandler unlatched the hood and raised it until it locked upright. He looked at the engine for a long time. Then he leaned in and felt the cables and tubes tangled throughout the compartment.

"Waste of time," Gibson said. He lay on the ground underneath the chassis and uncoiled another length of hose fitted to a high-pressure nozzle. He'd taken off his uniform blouse before crawling below in a grimy T-shirt. His arms were wet and white and bony and crusted with sand.

"Truck's just gonna get dirty again," he said. "Like everything else in this country."

Chandler nodded. But he knew army equipment functioned better when it was clean. He didn't know why except that it was true and he wanted this Humvee to do what it was designed to do.

"Spray the dirt that's packed in the wheel well," Chandler said. "While you're down there, check for cracks in the tie rods."

They worked outside in the shadow of the maintenance garage. It was a two-story metal hangar next to the fuel pumps and the gravel lot where the convoys staged. Inside, mechanics on rolling boards slid under gun trucks and armored semis. They twisted and contorted to reach the engines, scaled the vehicles in grease- and oil-stained coveralls worn unzipped with their sleeves tied around the waist. They turned wrenches and ratchets, sheared and fused, and their grinders and torches consumed the hangar with a whine of assembly and a blizzard of sparks that glowed dim on the smooth, oily concrete floor.

A fence topped with razor wire surrounded the hangar. Beside it was a plywood shack for air-conditioning repairs, a long building where the maintenance sergeants drank coffee and printed dispatch requests, a tin hut within a smaller, fenced-in lot filled with barrels and cans of motor oil and jugs of windshield-washer fluid. A nine-foot concrete barricade shielded everything from the fuel point. Along the slab were shipping crates where the spare parts were stored. Many wrecked vehicles. Gun trucks, up-armored flat beds, semis and fuel pods scorched or smashed by roadside bombs, rockets, and incendiary grenades. Some of the crew compartments reeked of melted skin.

Gibson crawled out from underneath the truck with a cigarette burning between his teeth. He slung the hose over the open driver's door then helped Chandler lower the hood and latch it down.

"Best 1114 in the platoon," Gibson said. "Never left the wire. Not since we've been here. Wrench jockeys tuned the shit out of her anyway. Like you asked."

Chandler lit a cigarette. He eyed a group of mechanics on break outside the maintenance bay. They slouched against the hangar wall, smoking or sipping Gatorade and Pepsi in the dense heat. A gang of pale, wiry, chinless men with blank eyes and faces tarnished with grease and sweat.

"You're tight with those guys," he said.

"They're my people," said Gibson. "You'd get along with them."

"Doubt it," Chandler said.

"Well. You know your gun trucks," said Gibson.

Chandler told him about how he'd worked at the factory where Humvees were built. Buggman's father was an executive at AM General and bamboozled them jobs after high school. He'd drive from Union, Michigan, in the cool morning dark across the Indiana state line to South Bend. He unloaded trucks delivering parts in the receiving dock, but sometimes roamed the plant and watched the assembly line.

"I'm no rivet head," said Chandler. "Now my old man. He's gonna drop dead trying to put in enough years to draw a pension."

"Kinda cars?" Gibson said.

"Tool and die man," Chandler said. "The plant where he works makes machines, and those machines make other machines and those machines make SUVs."

Gibson wiped the sweat and oil off his forehead with the back of his hand. He looked into the maintenance garage then put on his cap and spat. "Sounds familiar. Like the army," he said.

Chandler nodded and stamped out his cigarette. "Shower? Change your uniform yet?"

"No," Gibson said. "That makes about as much sense as washing this truck. After we got back, I dropped my gear, ate, then went to bed."

"Pass me the hose," Chandler said. "I'm gonna clean the inside."

"Get any sleep?" said Gibson.

"I'm OK," Chandler said.

"Really?" said Gibson.

"Did what I needed to do," Chandler told him. He squeezed the nozzle and sprayed down the seats and floorboards. He left the doors open so the interior would dry out in the heat. Murky water drained from the holes in the gun truck's floorboards. Gibson coiled the high-pressure hose and hung it on the pump.

Chandler rubbed his eyes then walked a lap around the vehicle, kicking the tires. He lit a cigarette. He inhaled deeply and a huff of smoke became lodged in his throat. His hands shook and he grabbed the side of the gun truck and pitched forward, gagging.

"Back in Ardmore," Gibson said. "They'd say you're eating soup with a fork."

"I was up late," Chandler said. "Couldn't sleep and something in my care package isn't agreeing with me now."

Gibson watched him and thumbed his Zippo open and shut. "Take a nap."

"Not done yet," Chandler said.

"All this is that important?" said Gibson.

"Yup."

"Least get off your feet for a little while."

"That's what the Percocet's for," Chandler said.

Gibson drew on his cigarette and blew smoke out his nose. "Trying to help."

"Help me by taking a shower," Chandler said. "And shave and brush your teeth and put on clean ACUs. Don't show up at formation looking like a meth head. Top and Sergeant Mack will get on my case."

"I'll park and lock the truck first," Gibson said.

Chandler crushed his cigarette under the heel of his boot then held out his hand.

"Keys," he said. "I'll take care of it. Gonna stop by the commo shop first."

"Lemme tag along. Please," Gibson said. "All I need is a real quick look at—"

"No."

CHAPTER ELEVEN

He stepped inside the communications shop and shut the door. Parker sat in a torn leather chair with her ankles crossed on the edge of her desk. A thin cigar smoldered between her ivory teeth. She'd molded her floppy hat in the shape of a fedora and pulled the brim to her eyebrows.

"These porno books are full of lies," Parker said. She shook a rolled magazine at a soldier named Ravi, who stood across the room, counting the radio headsets and cables strewn along the tiered wood shelves that lined the wall.

"*Maxim* isn't porn," said Ravi. "And I'm doing all right with the ladies."

"The Widow Makers aren't ladies," Parker said.

"Boss. Can't tell me that women don't like sex," Ravi said.

"Telling you the opposite," Parker said. "But you gotta understand, the thought of dick doesn't make our minds gushy. Try what they tell you in this magazine on the girls in my club. You're gonna get your Hindu ass in trouble."

"I'm from Albuquerque," Ravi said. "And, since we're being honest, there's other girly parts I wanna make gushy."

"Don't. Talk. Like. That," Parker said. She grinned and sucked on the cigar. A cylinder of ash fell and broke apart on her uniform blouse.

"Still got those condoms I gave you?" she said.

"Might," said Ravi.

"Walk your ass to the aid station," Parker said. "Now. Tell the medics I said to give you more. A lot more. Another Widow Maker convoy due in this afternoon. I'm not telling the chief anymore lies after you get infected with chlamydia again."

Parker knocked her boots together and exhaled a cherry-scented haze of smoke from her lips. She tapped the cigar into a forty-millimeter grenade casing filled with ash and crinkled cigarette butts and glared across her desk at Chandler.

"The fuck now?" she said after Ravi closed the door and they were alone.

"Need my radios squared away," Chandler said.

"Was that plural?" Parker said. "As in, more than one radio?"

"And a Duke," Chandler said. "Antennas, headsets, and a BFT. My gun truck's outside."

"Don't try to be funny," Parker said. "You totally suck at jokes."

Chandler lit a cigarette and palmed the burning end. "I don't know how to answer that," he said.

Parker swept an index finger at the door.

"Out with that nasty thing," she said. "Only person allowed to smoke in my shop is me."

Chandler stepped out and shut the door gently. He finished his cigarette on a wood bench near the gravel-paved vehicle queue where he'd parked the gun truck. He was thinking about Parker. She sat in her chair, her face pressed hard against him as he leaned on the corner of the desk. His fingers mashed and squeezed the top of her hat. The brim was level with his belt buckle. He smoked her cigar, watching Parker as she worked on him. Milking her fist like she'd done with the handset for the radio. He threw his head back, smiling as Parker unbuttoned her uniform pants and jammed her fingers between her thighs and groaned.

It was painful to sit. He dropped the cigarette butt in an empty ammunition can below the bench and limped to a port-a-john. He went in and sat down and lit another cigarette. He thought about making the ache go away but it was baking hot inside the toilet so he read the graffiti scrawled in pencil on the walls.

Chuck Norris once took a vacation to the Virgin Islands. Now they're called the Islands.
There is no theory of evolution, only a list of creatures Chuck Norris has allowed to live.
When the boogeyman goes to sleep at night, he checks his closet for Chuck Norris.

Only his legs hurt when he stepped out into the heat again. Parker knelt behind his gun truck. Her canvas tool bag lay unzipped on the gravel where she polished the copper threads on one of the radio antennas with a length of rope. She'd removed her uniform blouse and the sun shone on the back of her shaved head. Her T-shirt hugged her narrow shoulders and the straps of her sports bra. The large knife was on her hip. The sheath worn and handcrafted from a hardened swatch of animal hide that rested against the curve of her buttocks.

"Got to lube this shit up," Parker said. "Can't jam it in dry and expect it to work."

Chandler wiped his forehead with a sleeve and put on his cap. He put a hand in his pants pocket and pinched himself. "What to work?" he told her.

"The antennas," Parker said. She turned so Chandler could see the dab of silicone on the end of her finger. "Keep these connectors clean and lubricated and you'll get better reception."

He nodded and tried to focus on the sergeant's stripes sewn onto her hat. Her eyelashes fluttered and it was hard not to look at them.

"Aren't you hot?" Parker said.

"It's summer. In the desert," Chandler said.

"Don't wear your uniform," Parker said.

"Kinda hard to avoid," Chandler said.

"Wear PT shorts instead of pants. I would if they'd let me. But I'm a girl."

"It's best if I keep my pants on."

Parker flicked the silicone off her finger and looked at him. Then she leaned inside the truck and began to turn the dials on the pair of radios mounted between the driver and passenger seats.

"Rest of your squad was here this morning," she said.

"I believe it," said Chandler.

"Guys look like you're going to war."

"I'm a replacement," Chandler said. "Nobody tells me anything. When I first got here I had to find my own ammunition."

Parker clucked her tongue and climbed out of the gun truck.

"Well. Don't get blown up again," she said. "That's how you got the limp, isn't it?"

Chandler stood in the sun and blinked. He was thinking about how he should answer when Parker shook her head and reached into her tool bag and lobbed him a large tube.

"Silicone?" he said.

"So you'll get better reception," she told him.

Parker knelt and closed her tool bag. Then she rose and shrugged into her blouse and pulled the zipper up and over her teardrop-shaped breasts. Chandler felt the back of his neck warm when he saw her watching him.

"Corporal Chandler," she said.

"Sergeant Parker."

Chandler got in the driver's seat. He watched Parker take her tools inside the shop. She left the door open. After a while her hand reached out and grabbed the door latch and slammed it shut. He turned the ignition switch and waited until the glow plugs warmed and he could start the engine.

He drove the gun truck along the packed sand road that lapped the inner perimeter of the camp. He throttled the engine and sped for several meters then braked hard, gauging the distance needed to stop. He drove another lap and listened to the fan whirl under the hood as the engine heated up. By the third lap, he had to switch off the air conditioner to drive the vehicle at its top speed.

Best 1114 in the platoon, Chandler thought. We must've inherited some sorry ass trucks.

Near the main gate, he turned onto a side road skirting an embankment. He passed two sergeants from first platoon in a John Deere golf cart ferrying ice water and Styrofoam boxes with chow to the soldiers in the watchtowers. The small cart kicked up a cloud of dust. Out of the cloud sprinted Vogel. His T-shirt wet against his chest and biceps as he ran, oblivious to the heat and bright sun. He waved at the gun truck and ran faster.

Chandler kept driving. He drove past the landing pad for the helicopters until he reached an uninhabited section of camp that had been a holding area for detainees. He reversed and backed the gun truck against the dirt wall between two watchtowers. He switched off the engine and slid the window open. He looked across the empty sand lot at the barracks trailers in the distance, the trash dump and smoke from the burn pit, thinking. When it became too hot in the armored cab he opened the door and lit a cigarette. He took a long draw and exhaled slow, listening to the wind and the air conditioners churning in the watchtowers above.

He lit another cigarette. He'd been distracted by the letter and the death of Jim Eton but now he thought about Parker and if he'd done or said something embarrassing. He didn't know why he cared, but he did.

A dull thud as a shell exploded far out in the desert. The ground shook then the sirens blared inside the camp.

He closed the driver's door halfway and waited for another shell to land. Finally he got out of the gun truck. The spare tire was bolted to the back bumper and around the tire was a red plywood stop sign. Written on the sign in Arabic and English was, *Stay Back 100 Meters Or You Will Be Shot.*

He swatted the flies that tried to crawl into his ears and urinated on the stop sign.

Yup. You should've stayed back, Chandler told himself.

If he hadn't deployed, the spring semester at Michigan State would be ending soon and he might have spent that afternoon lying on the grass beneath the elms. A spot with a view of The Sower on Beaumont Tower's red bricks through the hanging leaves, birdsong and the girls bouncing to class along the walkway. He liked girls and he liked to look at them. The girls liked to drink at college and they liked that he did, too, even though when he drank it was for different reasons. He wanted to be with the girls but to do that he had to talk to them and pretend. Pretend he had something to talk about. Pretend he was interested in his coursework or sports or current events when none of it seemed to matter. Pretend he wasn't a billboard of the Hollywood veteran with a broken body and brain and no future.

And he was good at pretending. So good, that when he was activated from the reserves, he'd arrived at the replacement depot thinking he would hang long enough to draw a paycheck or two before he was mustered out and returned home. All he'd had to do was show the doctors the scars on his legs and feet and tell them about the pain. How he felt when he thought about what happened in the wheat field. But during his physical he'd remembered Dempsey, the guy who didn't want to quit even after he'd lost his thumbs in the ambush. About Sergeant Reed and Tran, what all three of them would've done if they'd still been alive and received orders to suit up and deploy one more time.

Those guys were the real soldiers, Chandler thought. Heroes. And you're just pretending you're not a sham.

Another shell exploded in the desert. He winced and listened to the sirens. He saw Vogel running on the dirt road as he rounded the curve and waved him towards the truck.

Vogel sprinted and met him at the hood. He was dripping sweat and his legs shook but he wasn't out of breath. "Someday," he said. "Hajji's gonna lob one of those rockets inside the wire. Fucking matter of time before he figures out the elevation."

"Not rockets," Chandler said. "Those were from an eighty-two millimeter mortar. And the heat's gonna kill you first."

Vogel shrugged and pulled off his T-shirt. He wiped his face then wrung the shirt in his fists. "It's maybe a hundred thirty today. Anyone can suck that up for three miles."

"Talked to the other platoons yet?" Chandler said.

Vogel nodded. "Word's spreading fast."

It was a mission swap. The Widow Maker company was relocating to take over as the camp security force. Golf Company would split up by platoon and escort the supply convoys traveling back and forth between Kuwait and Iraq.

"We'll be gypsies," said Vogel.

"More like roving targets," Chandler said.

"Don't care," said Vogel. "Can't stand this fucking camp anymore. Or the observation post."

The sirens stopped. The hot breeze blew across the camp. Chandler tapped a cigarette from his pack. He was thirsty and his hand shook. He lit up and exhaled hard against the wind.

"It's a good mission," said Vogel.

"We're gonna get blown up," Chandler said.

Vogel shrugged. "I want that CIB and Purple Heart."

"You don't get to choose," Chandler said.

"Choose what?"

"Never mind. Forget it."

Vogel looked at the crumpled pack of cigarettes and lighter on the hood of the gun truck. He looked for a long time then pulled a cigarette out and sniffed it before lighting up.

"Special occasion," he said.

They smoked and didn't talk. Finally, they climbed in the gun truck and drove back to the trailers. Vogel asked to be dropped at the Internet café. He was meeting Sundance, the interpreter, who wanted help setting his fantasy baseball roster.

"His pitching sucks," said Vogel. "I tried to tell him the ERA is everything. But that old Hajji refuses to start a southpaw."

"All our weapons and gear's squared away?" Chandler said.

Vogel nodded. "Waiting on you to give it a look."

Chandler cracked the window and flipped a burning cigarette outside. "Still really want to be a team leader someday?" he said.

"My mouth waters just thinking about it," Vogel said. He stared out of the passenger window.

Chandler glanced sideways as he drove, at Vogel's smooth brown skin and thick blonde hair. Keeps the genius hidden behind those black eyes, he thought. Has to. Gotta be a weakness for anyone who grows up in a neighborhood that's almost as dangerous as Iraq. Then he thought about his own childhood and how he was an outcast. How it'd felt to go back to the lake after Afghanistan with his spirit beaten to a pulp. It wasn't his fault but he did feel bad for blocking Vogel's promotion to sergeant and stealing his fire team and he wanted to make it up to him.

"Fine," Chandler said. "If you say we're OK, then we're OK."

"Finally. Someone who believes me," said Vogel.

Chandler shrugged. "What I believe is that we're all just one bullet or an IED away from our next promotion."

He let Vogel out at the Internet café. He drove the gun truck around the camp again and then parked near the Hajji Shop. He went in and bought seven cartons of cigarettes. He crossed the basketball court to the Java Shack. Then he sat on one of the picnic tables outside and sipped a cappuccino.

A supply convoy entered through the main gate. The armored Freightliners towed trailers loaded with steel shipping crates and pallets of water. One had an Abrams tank that was missing the barrel for the cannon. The gun truck escorts peeled off from the column and parked along the roadside.

Chandler looked at the gun trucks. The duffle bags and rucksacks covered in dirt lashed to the trunks, the black widow spider spray painted on the turret shields. A gunner climbed out of the cupola and stretched on the roof, her face tanned except for the pale mask where goggles had covered her eyes. She removed her helmet and shook loose a braid of auburn hair that fell onto a shoulder. She'd hung her body armor on the belt-fed grenade launcher in the turret. She unzipped her flight suit and tied the sleeves around her waist. She saw Chandler looking and smiled and cupped her apple-shaped breasts and wiggled them in her gloved hands.

"Like that?" she said. "Fucking Fobbit."

Chandler saluted with his coffee cup then stood and took the cigarettes back to his trailer. He set them on the poncho liner spread on his bunk. He looked at his watch. He wanted to check his e-mail and Facebook but he went to the laundry trailer instead. He waited outside in the line, smoking until the contractors unlocked the doors. He thought about the Widow Maker in the gun turret. About Parker and then about his dead friends, who couldn't talk to anyone. He decided it was OK that he wanted the chance to talk to Parker again.

CHAPTER TWELVE

He drove to the motor pool and inched the gun truck into its parking spot then locked the doors and the hatch in the turret.

The soldiers in second squad shuffled and scratched themselves in the rank they'd formed in front of the row of parked vehicles. Chandler took his place in the file beside Gibson. "Now you smell like someone's ass," he told him.

"I took a shower," Gibson said. "Changed my uniform, too. Even put on new socks."

"Actual ass this time," Chandler said. "Worse than usual. Seriously, it's terrible, man."

Witkowski held up the wedding ring on his right hand.

"My fault," he said. "I have lost weight. The band slipped off in the Port-a-John. I needed Gibson's long arms to get it back."

Chandler lit a cigarette, letting the smoke float in his lungs. He smoked half then stubbed it out. The coffee churned in his stomach. His shins throbbed and his hands shook as he felt in his pockets for a painkiller. He couldn't find one so he fingered the whistle instead.

Hurd was their platoon leader and he stood in front of the formation. He wheeled and called the squad to attention when the company commander emerged from between the buildings on the other end of the motor pool.

Captain Gavin Ingram massaged the base of his neck as he stepped from the walkway. He stopped and tore a memorandum off the bulletin board. He crossed the sandy lot like a minefield.

"Here comes the big green weenie," someone said.

"My cousin looked like that. Right before he had stroke."

"Nicotine's got him by the balls. Bummed a dip from me yesterday."

"Heard his wife's pregnant again."

"Ain't no way in hell he's the dad."

Mackenzie leaned forward and scowled down the rank and then it was quiet again. Hurd saluted and stepped to the rear of the formation, leaving Ingram alone in the hot breeze that blew across the motor pool.

He held up the memorandum and told them about the soldier who'd been raped. That everyone on the camp was to travel in pairs after dark. Lock the doors to their trailers. Report suspicious activity. Ingram cleared his throat. He told them about the orders changing their mission. He told them second squad second platoon had been picked for a special task: Act as scouts for the convoys, driving far out in front looking for ambushes and bombs planted along the route.

Mackenzie spat. "Sir. That's as wrong as two boys fucking."

"Had to pick someone," Ingram said.

"That's not an answer," said Mackenzie.

Ingram wadded the memorandum in his fist. He tugged the straps of the shoulder holster he'd bought at the Hajji Shop. The leather decorated with metal studs that gleamed in the bright sun.

"Volunteers," Ingram said. "All of you wanted combat. Right? This is your opportunity."

"Fuck combat," Mackenzie said. "We did our time. Guarded the FOB. Filled sandbags. Baked our dicks off stringing razor wire. Frisking the Smurfs. The motivation's been milked out of us. If anyone deserves to sham a little until it's time to go home, it's us."

"Be thankful you weren't extended three months," Ingram said.

Mackenzie's eye twitched. He hitched up the holster hanging low on his thigh.

"Regular army," he said. "Never admit it, but you couldn't run this war without the Guard and reserves, without people to do the shitty jobs. You wanna send us out onto IED Alley. Now? With five weeks left. It's bullshit. Sir."

Ingram raised his head, looking over and behind the row of soldiers. "This is done," he said. "As for what it is, maybe you're just worried about getting your old job back at the Wal-Mart."

Someone whistled. Then it was quiet and the wind picked up and sand scattered across the motor pool. Ingram flipped a salute and crossed the lot back to his desk inside the orderly room. After he'd gone, Mackenzie balled up his cap and flung it on the sand.

"You could go to the IG," said Hurd.

"Tell ya what I'm gonna do," Mackenzie said.

Humming behind the formation. The deep tone and rhythm reminded Chandler of a war chant from a black-and-white western he'd watched in the seventh grade.

Jesus Christ, he told himself.

Flowers stepped from between the gun trucks. He strode into view and faced the soldiers.

"First sergeant. We need to talk to you," said Hurd.

"Enlisted business," Flowers said. He hugged Hurd with one arm and steered him away from the formation. They spoke quietly for a long time and when it was done Hurd put a hand in his pocket and walked towards the trailers, shaking his head at the sky.

Flowers crossed his wrists in front of him and watched Hurd leave. Quiet except for the groan of the nearby generator that powered the orderly room. He licked the edges of his mouth. Then he stooped and snatched Mackenzie's cap off the ground. He slapped the cap against his leg and after he gave it back to Mackenzie he pushed a finger to his lips.

"Shush," he said. "Shut your dick garage. It's sad. Grown men sniveling like a bunch of little girls. I'll send Shorty to the PX. Tell him to buy tampons to plug all the bleeding pussies in this company."

Vogel bowed his head and moaned. "A countenance more in sorrow than in anger."

Flowers cocked his head and blinked. "You," he said. "Are not as smart or tough as you think you are. Where I come from we had more dogs than people. And more empty beer cans than both. Another peep and I will bend you over one of these trucks and fuck you in the ass. Right here. In front of all your sad friends."

Flowers waited in the quiet. After a long time, he stooped and picked a cigarette butt from the sand. He rolled the butt in his palm and stepped close and dropped it at Chandler's feet.

"Satisfied with your decision?" Flowers said.

Chandler shifted his weight, thinking.

"It's not a riddle," Flowers said.

Chandler looked at the soldiers. They slouched and stared at the sand or at the buildings or at him. He'd learned a little about them since he arrived. He had no clue as to the kind of men they were before the deployment. But now he thought he understood what they had become and why. That he shouldn't answer but he was going to anyway.

"I'm satisfied," he said. "You were right, top. I think too much. And I've been thinking a lot lately. This is a good unit here. We were good troopers in the airborne but those days are over for me. This is my squad now. And it's got what the active duty doesn't. Sergeant Sullivan. He's a Maine state policeman. Teasdale is a chef. Ash writes computer code and Nettles is a master carpenter. Yacoubian's a smoke jumper. Doc Karlskoga's gonna be a lawyer someday and Apple repairs bicycles. This entire company has got people with skills. Instead, the guys have sat in the towers, an empty building, in this heat. And now they're getting sent outside the wire to do a risky job. Someone might get blown up. I don't think anyone's unmotivated. They're frustrated. Captain Ingram just gave us a hard pill to swallow. It's a hard pill because at times like this the bosses don't act like they want to win the war. It's like there's someone flying a desk somewhere who wants to keep it going on and on for as long as possible. I think a guy like Ingram and maybe even you would really like that. And after what happened the other night out on the highway in front of that, whatever that thing is out there, I'm starting to think nobody cares if we all got shot to pieces."

Flowers ground a boot into the soft sand. He breathed deep and regarded Chandler and the rest of the soldiers with his narrow eyes. "Done?" he said.

"I'm done," said Chandler.

"You had an out," Flowers said. "In a way, all of you did and chose not to take it. I told you before. I don't give the orders. So what if the commander has it in for you? The insurgents have it in for you, too. Ingram thinks you made him look bad. He's petty. But he's also a got job to do. There might come a moment, Corporal Chandler, when you'll understand that. When you realize you can't afford to think of your comrades as men or soldiers or even human beings. When you simply have to think of them as resources."

CHAPTER THIRTEEN

AFTER THEY WERE DISMISSED Chandler walked to the chow hall beside Vogel, Gibson, and Witkowski. His shins and ankles were sore, but he stepped quickly across the sand and along the gravel path. He was very hungry.

"Resources," Vogel said. "Fucking classic."

"You all right?" said Chandler.

"Why wouldn't I be?" Vogel said.

"He was just messing with your head," said Chandler.

Vogel nodded.

"That's what loony people do," Vogel said. "When I was eleven, bunch of clockers cornered me after school and whipped me with a radio antenna off a car. Crazy first sergeant can't break me."

Chandler lit a cigarette and held it in his teeth. He removed the identification card from his wallet. "He's not crazy."

"Still. That man has problems," Witkowski said. "Problems that just became our problems."

Chandler shrugged and waved his cigarette in the air. He told them about Flowers and the things he'd done in Afghanistan. How the army was radically different when Flowers had joined. An army that'd trained its soldiers to slug it out with the Soviets in a stand-up fight.

"Flowers would level a whole city block to kill one bad guy," Chandler said.

"Never get away with that in Iraq," said Gibson.

Vogel sucked his teeth. "Ergo, the problem."

They waited in the long line that snaked outside the chow hall, behind dozens of other mumbling soldiers sweating in the cloud of humidity that washed across the camp at dinnertime. When they neared the entrance, Chandler and the others stopped at the metal drums half-filled with sand and made sure their pistols were unloaded, then showed their identification cards to a pair of sentries from Golf Company's third platoon.

"Fazio," Vogel told one of the guards. "This shit just keeps getting better and better."

"Asshole," Fazio said. "We got screwed again. We're babysitting convoys to Kuwait. Never gonna see any action. Never gonna get our CIBs."

Vogel smiled and punched his chest. "I'm headed north. You know I'm gonna get mine."

"Then pay me my money," Fazio said. "Don't try to get blown up so you can welch out."

"Money for what?" Vogel said.

"The Super Bowl," said Fazio. "Hester returned a kick for a touchdown, Manning played outside in the rain and the Bears still lost. Forget about 1985, it's over. Now pay me my money."

"Suck my dick," Vogel said.

They split up after rinsing their hands and faces in sinks by the door that sprayed scalding water from the faucets. The population of the camp had tripled since the start of the surge. Inside the large building, the chow hall was filled with noise and jostling bodies, blurred gray and black and brown and olive drab camouflage, angling and elbowing for a turn in one of the serving lines or the soda fountain or the dessert bar, for a seat at the folding tables jammed against the walls or neat in rows throughout the belly of the vast white-walled fiberglass dome.

Chandler carried his tray to the short-order line. He sidestepped until it was his turn, then he ordered a grilled cheese and onion rings and a hamburger from the Ugandan contractor busy scraping burnt curls of grease from the surface of the grill. He liked that his meals were different than they'd been in Afghanistan. The food in Iraq was good and there was a lot of it. The variety of the dishes not unlike to what he'd grown up eating. And because of this, a part of him felt as if they all were somehow condemned, sacrifices to the gods of war being buttered up for their last meal. Chandler shook his head and filled up a plastic mug with black coffee from one of the aluminum vats before joining the others at a table in the center, where the chow hall was most crowded.

"Those are new," he said, waving an onion ring at the plasma televisions mounted on the walls.

"Tired of CNN," Gibson said. "Mess sergeants ought to let us watch something cool, like Fox News, or the Weather Channel."

"What's so cool about the weather?" Vogel said.

"Storms," Gibson said. "Haven't seen rain in nine months."

"Loony people. Fucking surrounded," Vogel said, chewing a roast beef sandwich.

Witkowski ate ice cream from a small paper cup. He rolled his eyes and moaned, turning a stainless steel spoonful of vanilla upside down in his mouth before he licked it clean.

"You're gonna get gas," Gibson told him.

"A little taste," Witkowski said. "It'll help me feel better."

"Stop. I mean it," said Gibson. "You'll stink up the goddamned trailer."

Witkowski winked and tapped the spoon against the rim of the cup.

"Nothing in today's mail?" Chandler said.

"There's always tomorrow," said Witkowski.

"Pictures of your girls?" Chandler said. "That's what you're expecting?"

"Copies of the books," Witkowski said. "When I started Witkowski's Best Polish Cleaning, I wasn't much older than Vogel is now. I had a van and a strong back and a bucket of rags and a mop and some bottles of Simple Green. Now it's my slice of the franchise. America. Understand? I worry it'll all go to shit while I'm downrange."

"Economy's fine," Vogel said. "But wait. This time next year, you'll be gobbling the Ben & Jerry's by the gallon."

"Leave me alone," Witkowski said.

Laughing at the next table. Six Widow Makers hunched on the long benches, their empty plates and cups scattered in front of them. They hailed from an Army Reserve military police company based out of Nebraska and nearly all of them were female. There was talk on the camp, even a story in *Stars and Stripes*, about how that'd happened, if it was by chance or on purpose, but nobody knew for certain. Pretty girls in faded and stained olive drab or khaki jumpsuits, the sleeves rolled to their forearms. Faces cracked and tanned. Deep wrinkles at the ends of their blank eyes, which the sun had squeezed into a permanent squint. Reeking of diesel fuel and gunpowder. Their hair in bobs or pinned up tight but otherwise they all looked the same.

"Hi, Hector," said one of the girls.

"Sup," Vogel said. He jerked his chin and brushed three fingers through his thick hair.

"Susan," the girl said. "You wouldn't remember."

"I know who you are," said Vogel.

"I was Jessica's friend."

"Who?"

"Sergeant Hostetler. Jessica Hostetler."

Vogel scanned the chow hall. "Where's she at?"

The Widow Makers stopped laughing and fumbled with their cups.

"Landstuhl," another girl said after they were quiet for a long time.

"She was a lotta fun," said Vogel.

"Her truck got hit on MSR Titan. Flash fire and she was wearing her contacts. Lost most of her vision."

Chandler lowered his eyes and sipped his coffee and listened to the broadcaster on the TV.

"That's not the only thing that slut lost while she was over here." The Widow Makers laughed, cackling and slapping palms, pounding their fists on the table.

"This is our camp now," the girl named Susan told them. "Here until November. No more route recon and clearance. No more convoys to escort. No snipers to dodge and daisy chain EFPs and ambushes. We've earned this. Now we'll get to sham like you guys."

Gibson wiped a paper napkin across his bottom teeth. "Those towers get old real fast," he said.

Susan toyed with her earlobe and smiled at Vogel.

"We're not Fobbits," she said. "Our squad rolls out tomorrow. Gonna spent the night in an empty building out by the highway."

"The observation post," said Vogel. "Who'd you piss off? "

"Know about it?" she said.

"Not much to know," said Vogel.

"Is it chill?" she said.

"I'll tell you what's the what," said Vogel.

"I'd like that," she said. The Widow Makers smiled and nodded. They stood together and slung their rifles and carbines across their bodies like field soldiers. Then they gathered the plates and cups, wiping the crumbs onto the floor until the table was clean. Vogel rose with his tray and left with them.

Gibson watched them go. He'd ordered a plate of barbecue chicken wings and sucked the meat off a drumette. His eyes followed the squad of Widow Makers as they weaved through the chow hall, past the tiered carts where they stacked their trays to the swinging exit doors Vogel held open for them. When he was done, Gibson dropped the naked bone to his cardboard plate and smeared his face with the back of a hand.

"Those girls are whores," he said. "They shack up with anyone they want, whenever they want."

Chandler shrugged. He was trying to remember what each of the Widow Makers at the table had looked like so he could think about them later.

"FOB hot," Gibson said. He nodded at the other Widow

Maker squads eating in the chow hall. "Wait until those girls get back to the states. Poof. All ugly again."

"Imagine," Chandler said. "If it was the other way around and the men were outnumbered 20-to-1 by females."

"I'd never leave," Witkowski said.

"Bullshit," said Gibson.

"Pussy explosion," Witkowski said.

"You got a good thing back home," said Gibson.

Witkowski took the old photograph from the pocket of his cap. He looked at it and stroked it with a finger then turned it around. He pointed to his wife, Maryla, who was still beautiful, and Blanca, the clever and popular one, Edyta, very good at math and all the sciences and Stefcia, the most ambitious.

"That's Luiza," he said, tapping the photo. "My oldest. She's good at nothing."

"But she's your favorite," Chandler said.

Witkowski grinned. "Look at those tits and ass. Incredible."

Chandler sprinkled salt on his grilled cheese sandwich and stared at it before taking a bite. He listened to the murmur of the chowtime banter and muffled voice of the broadcaster on TV. The screen showed a video of a stretch limousine and camera flashes and stepping out were women he did not recognize but they were young and beautiful and famous because their parents had money.

"Sonofabitch," Gibson finally said.

It was dark and still very hot by the time he'd finished eating. Chandler walked alone to his trailer. He went in and switched on the overhead light and closed the door.

He was thinking about roadside bombs and how to spot them out the window of a moving gun truck. He didn't think it was possible if they were hidden. He'd seen one go off by the sedan out on the highway. At the replacement depot, he was shown PowerPoint slides of different types of bombs. Some were rigged from landmines like the one they'd found in the wheat field in Afghanistan. He thought about that and he was afraid.

He'd set the package from Judy Eton atop the cases of bottled water stacked in the corner. He took two bottles and opened one. He took a sip and swished it in his mouth. It was clean and cool and familiar on his tongue. But then he spat the water into the trashcan without swallowing and emptied the water bottle into his coffee maker and turned it on, watching as the carafe filled.

Chandler opened his wall locker. He set his large rucksack on the mattress. Beside it he laid out fatigues, socks and T-shirts, a towel and running shorts. He rummaged through the duffle bag under his bunk. He found the patrol sleeping bag, a waterproof sack, a poncho, and a heavy fleece sweater and arranged them on the bed.

He scratched himself then stepped out and smoked a cigarette in the darkness. He smoked another and went back inside, shaking and sweating from the nicotine and nighttime heat.

He replaced the batteries in his night-vision goggles and SureFire flashlight. Packed a pair of socks and a T-shirt in his assault pack. Fifty feet of rolled parachute cord, seven cartons of cigarettes, single packets of Starbucks coffee, sugar and creamer, Tang and Propel drink mix, a baggie filled with Motrin and Percocet tablets.

He looked in his first-aid pouch. He made sure the bandages were sealed. That he could cinch the tourniquet tight using one hand.

Chandler drank coffee from his canteen cup. He paced the room and filled his cup again.

He disassembled his carbine and arranged the components on the nightstand. He needed a dental pick to dig the sand out of the chamber. He pulled a bore snake through the barrel until the spiraled rifling gleamed. Used a shaving brush on the bolt and the extractor pins and springs, and the grit packed in the grooves of the red-dot optic, around the ejection port and flash suppressor.

He took the thirty-round magazines out of the ammunition pouches on his vest and the six others in the bandolier he carried in his assault pack. He thumbed out the bullets into his helmet then took the magazines apart to clean the springs inside.

Now he was shaking. Chandler went out. He smoked, stamping on the butt and dropping it between the wooden planks on the walkway. He went to the port-a-john at the end of the block. When he returned, Mackenzie stood inside the trailer. He leaned on the launcher for an anti-tank rocket, reading the letter from Judy Eton.

"Door was open," he told him.

"Taking a leak," Chandler said.

"I could've been the Ether Bunny," said Mackenzie.

"Got other things on my mind," Chandler said.

"Apparently." Mackenzie slid the letter back inside the box.

Chandler nodded at the long, green rocket launcher. "Is that for me?"

Mackenzie shook his head. He looked at the gear on Chandler's bunk. He stuck his hand in the helmet, filled with five-five-six ball and tracer bullets. He grabbed a handful and let the shells sift through his fingers.

"Hajji's not gonna stick around long enough to let you shoot all this at him," he said.

Chandler shrugged and filled his canteen cup. "Hope not."

"Check your people?" Mackenzie said.

"Soon," Chandler said.

"Wish I hadn't," said Mackenzie. "Teasdale and Nettles. Right now they're sitting in their underwear, goofing on cough syrup, playing Madden in the dark. Did you know they sleep in the same bed?"

"People are rattled," Chandler said.

"No reason to lose control," said Mackenzie.

"Plenty of reasons, boss."

Mackenzie's eye twitched. He sat on the edge of the bunk and rolled his shoulder. Then he told Chandler how his gun truck had driven over a pressure-plate rigged artillery shell during his first deployment in 2004. Snapped his collarbone when he was ejected from the machinegun turret. The vehicle tipped and slid into a canal. The driver and team leader couldn't escape from the crew compartment and drowned.

"Now it's my job to stick up for you guys," he said. "That's why I bitched at formation. But this shit doesn't bother me. I don't need a reason to be here. Don't care if the country's Karblakastan and we invaded because they sold oranges on Tuesday. I'm a soldier. And this is my business. This is what I do."

Chandler and Mackenzie didn't talk for a long time. They stared at the floor and at each other and the bare walls and then finally they laughed and they laughed until it hurt.

Later, Chandler walked in the dark along the walkway between the rows of trailers. His fingers tapped the handgrip of his pistol. He weaved between barricades and crossed the gravel lanes to the next block, headed to Vogel, Gibson, and Witkowski's trailer.

Two soldiers in jumpsuits whispered in front of the door. They were short and thin with narrow shoulders. Females, Chandler thought. They turned and put out their cigarettes when his boots creaked on the wooden planks.

"Supervisor," one of them said.

"Shit," said the other.

They backed away from each other and hopped into the shadows between the trailers. Chandler watched them go, listening to the music bleeding from inside the trailer. He couldn't distinguish the lyrics or instruments. He only felt the methodical rhythm coursing through the boards under his boots.

The trailer door opened. A pulsing red light spilled onto the walkway. Inside, glow sticks had been sliced open and the fluorescent liquid splashed onto the walls. The yellow and green streaks changed colors in the light from a pilot's emergency beacon flashing in a corner. The strobe revealed the shadows of the girls dancing within, their shapes like ghouls writhing large and serpentine on the walls.

Gibson was naked. He sat in the small space between the bunks. His pale flesh bound to a lawn chair with duct tape. The Widow Maker from the chow hall named Susan balanced at the foot of one of the beds wearing unlaced boots. Her crotch was level with Gibson's face. Beefy nipples straining against a sports bra that'd been washed too many times, hips rocking in a pair of what looked like Witkowski's boxer shorts. She arched her back to take a long drink from a bottle of shampoo. She swallowed and wiped her hand across her mouth then balled up a fist and boxed Gibson on the ear.

"Make it clean," she said. "Make it clean again."

Vogel stumbled out wearing sandals and a condom. He shut the door as Gibson shrieked. Vogel squinted at Chandler standing in the darkness. He laughed and rolled off the condom and jammed it into an empty water bottle then urinated on the walkway.

"The fuck you want?" he said.

"Do you know who you're talking to?" Chandler said.

"I do now."

Chandler lifted his cap to rub his forehead. "I can smell the tequila and pussy," he said.

Vogel laughed again. His white teeth shone in the dark.

"You get caught," Chandler said. "Christ, if Flowers finds out."

"He'll do what?" Vogel said. "Tell the commander it was a great idea to pick us for route recon? I don't need a refresher on general order number one. No booze, no sex, no porno, blah, blah, blah."

"We're rolling out tomorrow night," Chandler said. "It could get ugly. Seriously ugly out there."

"That's why we're having a party," Vogel said.

Chandler pinched the bridge of his nose. He peered into the shadows along the length of the block until he knew they were alone.

"Fine," he said. "Screw the pooch outside the wire, get someone killed, or worse. That happens, I'll shoot you, Hector. In the head. Seriously. I'll pull out my pistol and I'll blow your brains out."

"Wanna get a piece of this?" Vogel said. He jerked his chin at the trailer door.

Chandler shook his head. He left Vogel standing in the darkness, smoking as he walked back to his trailer. Inside he sat on the edge of his bunk and pressed his hands together until they stopped shaking. He changed into his shorts and sneakers and went to the showers. There was a wait and he was gone a long time. The shower nearest to his trailer had three stalls. In one stall, the nozzle was missing. A soldier or a Smurf on cleaning detail had defecated in the other. When he finally returned he stood inside his cool trailer, looking at the weapons and gear spread across the mattress.

Chandler packed his rucksack and assault pack. He assembled his carbine then loaded the magazines with twenty-eight shells each to avoid wear on the springs. He took his knife and snapped open the blade. He tested the edge by shaving off a few of the dark hairs on his forearm. He looked at everything again and when he was satisfied got Sergeant Reed's whistle out of the nightstand. He tied the lanyard to his ammunition vest and knotted it so the mouthpiece hung above his first-aid pouch.

He went out and stood on the walkway and lit a cigarette, thinking as the smoke curled up and vanished into the night.

CHAPTER FOURTEEN

He was still smoking when a silhouette stepped onto the walkway between the trailers, into the shadows where the starlight was dim. Chandler palmed his cigarette. He held his hand over his nose and exhaled. Boot steps drumming on the wooden planks as the figure appeared to glide towards him. The distance closed and revealed the rumpled outline of a floppy hat, baggy fatigues, and the barrel of a carbine slung behind the back.

That's a girl, Chandler thought, after he saw the narrow, rounded shoulders. A large knife, the blade fat and curved, dangled from one hand. He relaxed his grip on the cigarette and huffed. The silhouette froze as the smoldering tip glowed then veered to where Chandler stood beside his door in the heat and darkness.

"Sergeant Parker," he said, backing away until he was no longer within the reach of the blade.

"Corporal Chandler," Parker said. "I almost totally fucked you up."

"I'm already fucked up," he said. "That was a joke."

Parker widened her stance on the planks. "The hell you doing out here?"

"Having a smoke," he said.

"You're not funny," Parker said.

Chandler tapped his knuckles on the thin plastic door. "This is where I live."

"This whole block," Parker said, "is for officers and senior NCOs. And you're neither."

"There's an answer to that," he said. "I'm not supposed to tell anyone."

Parker cocked her head and waited.

"When I got here," Chandler said. "There were no vacancies in the enlisted trailers. The guy who I replaced, his bunk was filled, too. I lived three months in the transient tents, until the billeting officer assigned me to this."

Parker exhaled. "I'm tired and too hot for this bullshit."

"I'll prove it," said Chandler, turning the key he'd left hanging in the lock. He swung back the bolt and cracked the trailer door. Light poured out. He thought Parker's lips might have been creased into a smile, but he'd quickly shut the door again and couldn't be sure.

"This camp has a shortage on privacy," Parker said. "A lot of people would complain if they knew a corporal was living alone."

"Only my chain of command knows about this," Chandler said. "And there's a catch. If another officer shows up and needs a room, I'm homeless again."

"Where would you go?" she said.

"Probably set up a cot in the company supply room," he said. "I won't go back to the transient village. At least until someone else in a trailer got whacked, then I'd hijack their bunk."

"You'd sleep in a dead person's bed?" Parker said. "You don't think that's a bit morbid?"

"A lot of things I'd do for a working air conditioner," Chandler said. "And besides, not everyone who gets hit gets killed."

"Uh-huh," Parker said.

They stood without speaking in the heat and dark. Chandler's cigarette had burned to the filter. He stamped it out and nudged it with his toe between the gaps in the planks and lit another.

"Whatcha got there?" Parker said.

"*Gauloises*," said Chandler. "They're foreign. The Hajji shop sells them."

"Let me try one," she said.

He held out the pack of cigarettes. His eyes adjusted to the darkness and he saw that Parker cradled a Styrofoam box, the kind used to deliver chow to the soldiers in the watchtowers. She set the box on the planks and took a cigarette while her other hand tapped the blade of the knife against her thigh.

Chandler hit the striker on his lighter. There were bursts of sparks as he flicked his thumb until the flame lit. Parker's pupils shrank from the sudden brightness. She reached for his hand, guiding the flame to the cigarette in her lips. Parker inhaled and puffed, extinguishing the light, returning them to the shadows.

"Nasty," she said. "Tastes like pencil shavings."

"They're real popular in France," Chandler said. "I had to smoke a few cartons before I got used to the burn."

"Why smoke them at all?"

"They're fifty cents a pack," he said. "If you know where they sell American cigarettes for five bucks a carton, don't hold out on me."

His legs hurt and he shifted his weight to the balls of his feet. He'd never stood this close to Parker before. In her boots and hat, the top of her head was almost level with his shoulder. His cheeks and base of his neck warmed after he smelled the trace of coconut soap that lingered from her last shower.

"I was just having a smoke," Chandler said. "Wasn't trying to creep anybody out."

"People get shot like that," Parker said. "Waiting like some hoodlum by the ATM."

"Or stabbed with a giant knife," he said. "That's how I knew it was you."

Parker turned her wrist so Chandler could see the flat edge of the blade. The steel widened from the hilt, extending into a crescent. "This," she said, "is not a knife. This is a *khukuri*."

"Whatever it is, it's bad ass," Chandler said.

"Belonged to someone else," Parker said. "But I like it. It's always with me."

"I got a knife, too," he said. "I don't carry it around like I'm trying to start trouble."

Parker slid the khukuri into the sheath on her belt.

"Camp commander issued a memorandum," she said. "After that guy was attacked. All females have to carry a knife or a bayonet at night. Even though everyone's got an M-4 or an M-9, we'll get written up if we don't have a knife."

"Missed that memo," Chandler said.

"You've got a dick," Parker said. "Doesn't apply to you."

Chandler looked at his running shoes. "Not scared of the Ether Bunny, or whatever he's being called this week?"

"Not convinced he's a he," Parker said. "Anyway, the knife thing is just more nonsense someone thought up for damage control. It's a lot easier to fix that problem than, gee, I dunno, maybe stop the Hajjis from lobbing rockets and mortars at the camp."

"Watch," Chandler said. "There'll be another memo that makes everyone wear reflective belts at night, like they do up north at Camp Gotham."

Parker laughed. "That was funny. You made a joke."

"I was serious," Chandler said.

"Still funny," she said. "Here, I can't smoke any more of this."

Chandler dropped his cigarette between the planks and took Parker's. He tasted strawberry from where she'd had her lips on the filter. A bead of sweat rolled down his spine.

"What's in the box?" he said.

"Midnight chow," Parker said. "I live on the other side of the next block. Sometimes I cut through here on the way to my trailer. I was going to eat and try to relax."

"Smells good," he said.

Parker pulled an oval-shaped flashlight the size of a thumb from her pocket, opened the container's lid and shined a thin beam inside. "Sausage links and hash-brown patties," she said.

"I like breakfast," Chandler said. "Especially late at night."

Parker closed the box. The white light shone onto the planks and Chandler's shins, the old wounds exposed in his running shorts. "Knew it. You got blown up," she said.

He swallowed a sour gel in his throat and tried to sidestep the beam that illuminated his legs, pockmarked with dime and nickel-sized scars from the ankles to the knees. Parker followed his movement with the light and knelt for a closer look.

"They got you real good," she said.

"Yup," Chandler said.

"Get a Purple Heart?" said Parker.

"My consolation prize," Chandler said.

Parker reached out with the little finger on her hand. "What's it feel like?" she said.

"Don't touch it, please," he said. "The inside feels like concrete and stiff all the time. Outside, where the skin is brand new, touch that and it's like static electricity. Makes me shiver."

"I think it looks cool," Parker said.

"Sure."

Parker turned off the light. He was glad it was dark again and neither he nor Parker could see his legs. He thought about saying goodbye, telling her a lie that he had to use the latrine then walking off until she'd gone. Before he could, Parker removed her hat and grabbed his hand and pressed his fingertips a few inches above her left temple.

The lump was firm. Chandler ran his middle finger along the length of her scalp. He traced the scar and guessed it was four inches long. In the dark, he imagined a centipede cutting across the stubble on her skull. He hummed as he drew his hand away.

"Feel that?" Parker said.

"Never noticed it before," Chandler said. "That why you shave your head?"

"I do that because it's hot," she said. "And low maintenance. Speaking of maintenance. I heard you're gonna be escorting convoys now. That's lousy. Suppose you won't be bothering me at the shop for a while?"

Chandler shrugged. "Don't know when I'll be back."

She stepped closer. "You smell wet. Take a shower? Get yourself clean?"

Chandler nodded. "I was going to chill out and drink coffee before I tried to get some sleep."

"What kind of coffee?" Parker said.

"The good kind," he said.

"I like coffee," Parker said. "Especially at this time of night."

"I can give you a packet."

"I got a different idea."

Parker opened his trailer door and stood in the light that shone from inside.

"Wait," Chandler said.

"My trailer sleeps six," Parker said, stepping through the door. "Never quiet. The lights are always on. Surrounded by five other girls and all their stuff."

"It's not allowed," he said. He stepped back but she pulled him inside.

After it was over they lay in his bunk under the poncho liner. The nylon fabric soft and cool against the warm bodies coiled together. Parker snaked into the crook of Chandler's arm, her head lazy on his collarbone. She ran her fingernails across the rise and fall of his stomach.

The overhead light was off and he stared at the darkness. The hum of the air conditioner drowned out their breathing. He held her waist, where the hourglass curved between the ribs and the slope leading to where she was smooth and round and firm.

"You awake?" Chandler said.

Parker's cheek nodded against him.

"I want to apologize," he said. "Earlier, you took me by surprise."

Parker rolled and rested her chin on the edge of his chest. "Never hooked up with a black girl before?" she said.

"Thought there'd be more kissing," Chandler said. "I've never done anything like that. I've done it before but not that way. Didn't think I ever would've. Not with anyone the way we just did. Especially not while I was in Iraq."

"Seen you watching me," she said. "Know you thought about it."

"Probably."

Parker turned her head and scratched her nose against his shoulder.

"Gonna be honest," she said. "Before tonight, I pegged you for the bible-study type."

Chandler kissed the top of her head. The stubble tickled his upper lip. He pulled her close with one hand, sliding the other behind his neck, to feel the warmth of her breath against him.

"Jim and Judy Eton," Chandler said. "They were Lutherans. You could say that's a light-beer version of Catholic. But they never made me go to church."

"There's no Mr. and Mrs. Chandler?" Parker said. "You know. Mom and dad?"

Chandler put his hand on Parker's shoulder. He clutched her tight in his palm then ran his hand down her arm and laced their fingers together, clasping her to him.

He told her how the Etons were his foster parents, the last ones. His mother was sixteen when she'd gotten pregnant by a man who already had a wife and two children. He told her about the breakdown his mother had had before she'd left for good, growing up in the foster homes and the letter that came with the care package. Then he told her about the day they found the landmine in the wheat field in Afghanistan.

"You were right," Chandler said. "I don't know much. Figured I'd join the Army and get some payback for 9/11 and ended up getting my ass kicked. And I'm afraid. Afraid I'll make the wrong call and get someone killed. I might even do everything right and that could still happen. I just want to bring my people home. Silly.

But if I could do that one thing, I dunno."

Parker rolled from under his arm and onto her back, her shoulder touching his.

"Too much. Sorry. I don't talk about it to a lot of people," he said.

"My first deployment," she said. "Fourth infantry. This place was wild back in 2003. We lost a few. That's when I was wounded."

Chandler blinked at the darkness and shrugged.

"Pecan pie," she said. "I was in the mess tent when there was incoming. Instead of going outside to the bunker, I turned around and went to the dessert table. *Katyusha* rocket hit in front of the exit, in the crowd. A tiny piece of shrapnel sailed through the gaggle and tagged me where it did."

Parker knocked her knuckles against her skull.

"You might've gotten killed," Chandler said. "That pie probably saved your life."

"Or if I'd ducked under the table," she said. "I wouldn't get migraines every two or three days."

Parker lifted his wrist and pressed a large button on his watch. Chandler didn't look at the time. He looked at her eyelashes fluttering in the aqua-colored light.

"How does that story, about how you got wounded, go over at home?" he said.

Parker answered in a high-pitched rasp. "*Wasn't any parade for me after Vietnam. The hippies threw garbage at us at the airport.*"

Chandler smiled. He smacked his gums and imitated the voice. "*And I spent three years in a Japanese prison camp. My generation didn't need a 'thank you.' We saved the world.*"

They laughed about that and then they lay quiet.

"Don't mean nothing," she said. "I'm a lifer. I know I'll be back in Iraq in a year, maybe two. Might even go to Afghanistan. There's nothing for me in Sarasota anymore. But you could go back to college. Or home. Anywhere."

Chandler moaned and shook his head.

"School, maybe," he said. "Worse case, I go back to the lake and find my old apron at the grocery, spend the rest of my life selling lunch meat and beer and chips to the tourists."

"What do you want?" she said.

Chandler shrugged. "I'm driving in a fog. It's hard to see what's beyond the headlights."

Parker reached for Chandler's watch again and pressed the button for the light.

"Time to go?" he said.

"Time to go."

He felt the mattress rise as she crawled from under the poncho liner and sat on the edge of the bunk. Their scents mingled in the trailer's chilled air, coconut and strawberry and sweat-soaked boots and wool socks and lust. He could barely make out Parker's shape in the dark as she stood and began to rummage the floor for her clothes. He lay on his side and tried to watch her.

"My name's Larry," he said.

"Nice to meet you, Larry Chandler," said Parker. She sat on the bunk and began to lace her boots. "Amanda."

"And after you walk out that door," he said. "We'll go back to being Sergeant Parker and Corporal Chandler?"

He felt her slide across the mattress until she was on top of him, clenching her knees tight around his hips. She pressed her mouth against his, gentle and cruel, and held it there until finally she got up and stood at the side of the bed.

He listened as Parker turned on her heel, grabbed her carbine from where she'd leaned it against his locker. He stared at the wall while she slung the short rifle behind her back. The door to the trailer swung open and on the wall Parker's shadow appeared taller and disfigured in the dim light. She drew the Khukuri and pulled the door shut as she stepped out, jiggling the knob to make sure it was latched.

When he knew she was gone, Chandler switched on the lamp that was clipped to the metal headboard. He sat on the edge of the mattress and surveyed the room and after a long time got up and locked the door.

Chandler pulled on his running shorts. The Styrofoam box remained under the bunk where Parker had left it. He sat and opened the lid and bit into one of the sausage links. He examined it, cold and wrinkled and gray. He took another bite and dropped the sausage in the box. Then he picked the condom off the floor and put that into the box with the wrapper and put everything in the trash can.

Chandler put on his T-shirt and lay down. When he began to feel tired, he leaned over and took his Beretta from the drawer in the nightstand. He dropped the magazine and checked to see it was loaded with twelve shells before he slapped it back in the handgrip. He pulled the slide and let it snap forward and listened to the ratchet tone of a bullet locking in the chamber. He thumbed the safety and watched the hammer fall.

He set the pistol on top of the nightstand and rotated the barrel to aim it at the trailer door before turning off the lamp.

CHAPTER FIFTEEN

They loaded the gun trucks and left Camp Tucson at sunset. The soldiers barely spoke as they rolled past the watchtowers into the corridor of blast barricades to the exit gate. Beyond the earthen rampart and razor wire, second squad drove along the trail cutting across the desert. The sky inhaled the swirl of dust spun up by the tires. It was dark by the time the patrol arrived at the highway. The four vehicles swung onto the northbound lanes and accelerated as they passed the concrete building and the burned out wreckage of the sedan.

Chandler cracked the door window and pushed out his cigarette. The burning tip tumbled into the heap of trash at the roadside. The armored cab was dark within except for the instrument lights glowing green on the dashboard and radios. He fingered the whistle and leaned towards the windshield. It was like riding the bus on his first day at a new school and he was nervous.

"I could walk faster," Gibson said over the truck's intercom. "Keep going this speed and Lieutenant Hurd and the main convoy's gonna pass us up."

Vogel shone a hand-held floodlight into the desert. He switched it off and lowered his night-vision goggles then sat in the turret behind the heavy machinegun, swaying on a canvas seat.

"The Widow Makers told me the deal," he said. "Route recon never finds the IEDs. The IEDs find us first. We'll make better time once we stop acting like a bunch of scared little girls."

Then it was quiet except for static in the headsets and

Witkowski snoring in the back seat. The headlights drilled through the smoldering darkness. Behind them, flares from the refineries across the Kuwait border shrank and submerged as they drove beneath the bridge at Al Safwan.

They refueled at Tallil air base then parked outside the chow hall, waiting for the supply convoy to arrive and unload its cargo. Chandler stayed with the gun trucks while the soldiers ate. He paced the lot in the dim morning light until the soreness left his legs. A *muezzin* sang through a loudspeaker and the sun rose from behind the Ziggurat of Ur. They finished eating and drove to the ancient pyramid. The patrol lapped it twice before parking their trucks beside the mud façade and one of the mammoth staircases ascending to the summit.

Vogel hopped out of the gun cupola. He walked to the great steps and knelt beside them. He placed a palm gently against the chipped tan bricks, as if they might collapse, and smiled for Witkowski's camera.

Gibson stretched in the driver's seat, watching. He lit cigarettes and gave one to Chandler, who leaned on the hood, drinking cold coffee from his thermos. He held the cigarette in his lips and nodded at the horizontal bullet patterns snaking across the long wall.

"Really shot this thing up," Chandler said.

"With a lot of different calibers," said Gibson. "Some of those holes were put there a long time ago."

Chandler nodded. He thought about the observation post and what they'd found the last time they were there.

"Why would anyone do that?" said Gibson.

"Someone thought it was important," Chandler said.

"Then why build it in the first place?" said Gibson.

"Because someone thought it was important."

Gibson blew smoke through his nose. He leaned out of the hatch and spat on the sand.

"Don't make no sense," he said.

"No," Chandler said. "No sense at all."

They smoked and looked at the ziggurat until Mackenzie blared the siren on his truck. The soldiers mounted their vehicles and the patrol rolled out of the gates to continue scouting for another armored caravan.

They drove, the gun trucks lumbering northwest into the desert. The sand rippled in little waves and glistened in the bright sun. They passed abandoned villages of walled houses. Crossed the Tigris and tributaries feeding into a vast plain lush with trees and shrubs, green grass in fields with herds of goats and cattle with bony necks and frothing jaws that gawked as the trucks rolled slowly by.

They waved at the animals. They waved at detachments of British and Czech and Polish soldiers posted at checkpoints along the highway or on the bridges, lounging atop armored cars, bleaching their hair in the sunshine. They waved at Iraqi youngsters who sprang from the ditches beside the canals, chasing the trucks in rags and sandals, hands clawing at the dust and if they ran too close the gunners pelted them with water bottles filled with urine so the children wouldn't be crushed under the tires.

The patrol rolled through a vacuum. A swath of desert where sand and highway stretched endless towards the horizon, as if the Earth itself dared them to drive their gun trucks off the edge of the world.

Chandler squinted through the dust covering the windshield. He was tired and the red stop sign lashed to the trunk of Mackenzie's gun truck was blurred. He could only make out: *Or You Will Be Shot.* Water droplets from the air vent splashed onto his boot. It was very hot in the armored compartment. The sweat burned his eyes, glued the rubber pads on his headset to the skin around his ears. He smelled himself and the odor made him dizzy. The drone of the engine was drowned out by a voice in his head repeating: *Or You Will Be Shot. You Will Be Shot.*

He blinked and squeezed the whistle hanging from his vest. He opened up the ice chest in the back seat. Witkowski slept beside the cooler, chin bobbing on the chest plate in his body armor. Slobber trickled onto the camera he cradled in his lap. Chandler fished in the icy water for a can of Red Bull and popped the tab and gave it to Gibson.

"Need a break?" he said.

Gibson shook his head, steering with his wrist draped over the wheel. He emptied the can then licked the rim.

"You can switch with Witkowski," Chandler said.

"Let him sleep," Gibson said. "What I want is for Vogel to stop reading that book and do his job. The pages are rattling in my ears and it's driving me nuts."

"Turn off the intercom," Vogel said. "No one else is complaining."

Chandler lit a cigarette. The smoke curled up and was sucked out through the turret. "He's right. Supposed to be looking around up there."

"Nothing to look at," Vogel said. "There's nobody out in this wasteland, not even the flies."

Chandler exhaled a lungful into the windshield. "Let me see the book," he said.

"You'll take it," said Vogel.

"I'm not gonna keep it," Chandler said.

Vogel dropped a paperback between his knees into the crew compartment. Chandler looked at the cover. He flipped to the middle and read a few lines then smelled the old pages.

"Any good?" he said.

"Not really," said Vogel.

"OK, then." Chandler cracked his window and nudged the book into the desert outside.

The patrol finally stopped near the city of Al Kut to rest and rendezvous with the convoy. The soldiers were billeted in a canvas tent at Camp Atlanta and after showering Chandler lay on a cot in the heat and dark, waiting until it was quiet. He shut his eyes and slid his hands under the waistband of his running shorts. He thought about Parker. The curve between her breasts and she was dancing. She danced for him, wearing a white bra and panties, gyrating hard against his lap. But he was so very tired and fell asleep before she finished.

They drove past Nippur to escort fuel trucks to Camp Cleveland. The highway bordered by tall grass and canals and there were many three-sided mud huts and shacks erected from cut brush. Inside these roadside stands stood shelves lined with cookies and canned juice, batteries and cell phone cards. Men in robes and slicked hair sat at tables outside. They smoked hookahs and sipped chai steeped in brass kettles, waiting on barefoot boys to scrub their jalopy cars and trucks with water ferried from the ditches in buckets. Bedouins whipped the columns of camels trekking to the markets. Iraqi policemen in blue lapelled shirts and creased pants at sandbagged checkpoints beneath each of the underpasses. Here the road became pockmarked with jagged craters. Black motor oil stains where gun trucks hit by a bomb coasted a few feet before they'd stopped and burned with the crews locked inside.

They reached Baghdad on the third day and were told to wait a few more until the next convoy. Camp Gotham was the largest of several compounds that surrounded the international airport. The platoon was quartered in a warehouse across the boulevard from a massive citadel that appeared to float in the middle of a man-made lake.

"That's where they run the war," Mackenzie told them.

"I'm gonna check it out," said Vogel.

"There's nothing left to steal," Mackenzie said.

"What about the lake?" Chandler said.

"Stocked with trout and catfish," Mackenzie said.

"If you need me, I'll be fishing," Chandler said. "Gotta be someone on this FOB who'll let me borrow their rod."

Mackenzie's eye twitched. "Leave it alone," he said. "They used to execute Shias and dump them in the water. Did that for decades. The fish ate the corpses. Now they're mutated."

His first full day at Camp Gotham, Chandler rode the air-conditioned shuttle ferrying soldiers and contractors to the linked compounds and the main PX. The bus drove him past the remnants of Saddam Hussein's empire and he'd get off to see the crystal ball palace, the boathouse, and the death to the infidel palace or to walk alone, thinking, in the shade of the fig trees planted along the avenues.

After he'd seen what he wanted to see, he boarded the bus simply to ride and listen to the passengers. They complained about the veal sautéed in lemon pepper the chow hall served at dinner, how the mineral water gave people kidney stones, the rash of syphilis at the dental clinic. He was angered at first at how well they had it compared to life on Camp Tucson. He knew it was a silly jealousy and soon his daily routine included long cold showers and naps and cheese omelets thick with ham, onions and mushrooms. Once, he spotted a group of paratroopers from his old regiment and thought he'd recognized one of them but he was wrong. He stopped at an Internet café, housed in what'd been a bathhouse for regime bureaucrats, and logged onto Facebook to update his status.

Larry Chandler is in bizarre-o world, he wrote.

They sat on a blast barricade in front of the warehouse. The ground shook as a shell burst over the headquarters palace, illuminating the darkness and raining shrapnel into the lake.

"MPs wrote me a fucking ticket," Vogel said. "Walked out of the gym and there they were. Mopes told me I gotta wear a reflective belt after dark."

Chandler sipped the cinnamon latte Witkowski had brought him. "What'd I tell you?"

"Can't believe this bullshit," Vogel said.

"Buy a PT belt at the PX," Chandler said. "Since you're going, pick me up four cartons of cigarettes, anything but menthol. Here's some cash."

Gibson winced as another shell boomed in the darkness.

"Snipers can see over the wall," he said. "Was in the barber shop yesterday when some dude got nailed outside on the basketball court. He went for a layup and took one in the face."

"Afterward," Witkowski said. "They cut the Internet. I was fighting with Maryla on instant messenger when the connection was turned off. They do that when someone dies. Always, that woman gets the last word. Always."

Another shell landed in the lake and exploded beneath the water. Moonlight shone on the pale fish that floated to the surface.

"Camp Tucson," Chandler said. "Bad food and crappy Internet and that landfill smell and I can't wait to get back."

"Then we'll go home," said Gibson.

Chandler nodded and drank his coffee. He'd almost forgotten their tour would end in roughly twenty-eight days and he thought about that and when he might see Parker again.

"Looked inside that palace," Vogel said. "Had to go with that idiot Lazlo, but I knew I'd find a way to scope out the Al Faw while I was here."

"What'd Lazlo take?" Chandler said.

"Door knob."

"Anything for yourself?"

Vogel shook his head. "They got nothing going on in there."

Their new orders came the next day and they left Camp Gotham. The patrol continued to clear routes for the supply convoys headed to the camps and outposts in villages and deserts south and east of Baghdad. One time, they rolled through a slice of Sadr City and another time they drove close to Ramadi. They never encountered insurgents but they knew they were there, passing other patrols and convoys stopped on the highway, waiting for a wrecker or dust-off, smoldering vehicles torn apart from bomb blasts or riddled by automatic weapons fire.

They fired tracer rounds at Iraqi drivers who veered too close or rammed the cars off the road, and sometimes they slowed and shot their machineguns into boxes or random bags of trash or discolored lumps of sand alongside the highway.

Outside of Balad Ruz, they shut down the road and established a cordon after they drove upon a dead heifer lying on its side in the median. The soldiers doused the cow with aviation gas and set it off it with thermite grenades. For nine hours they poured on more fuel and roasted the flesh and organs until the bones showed. They drove off once they were sure no one could plant an IED inside the carcass.

They found their first bomb the next day. Mackenzie spotted the gray Styrofoam tube in the thick reeds lining a roadside ditch. It was an explosively formed projectile, designed to punch a hunk of molten copper through a vehicle's armor and shower the crew inside with splinters of shrapnel. They backed off the gun trucks and set up a cordon. They sweated in their vehicles and looked at the device through binoculars, waiting for the engineers to arrive and blow it in place.

The demolition team was British army. Their lieutenant had red eyes and sores along his forearms that looked as if worms had burrowed out of the flesh.

"That a Blues and Royals patch?" Vogel said. He'd gotten Witkowski to take his place in the turret and he was breathing hard after running to where the lieutenant talked with Mackenzie and Chandler.

The British officer nodded and grinned sheepishly.

"The Coronet Wales," Vogel said. "Did he come? Is he with you?"

The lieutenant looked around and picked at the sores on his arm. "Harry?" he said.

"That's right," Vogel said.

"I believe he missed the party."

"Are you sure?" Vogel said.

"Well, I don't see him here now." He looked at Chandler and waved the flies off his arms.

"He just wanted to see the prince," Chandler said.

"Why would anyone want to do that?" the lieutenant said.

"Ever seen a prince before?" Chandler said.

"No."

"Me neither," Vogel said. He walked slowly back to the gun truck and sat atop the roof, waiting with Witkowski's camera to shoot video when the bomb was finally detonated.

Six days since they'd left Camp Gotham. They drove and Chandler was hot and bored and often he was frightened but he tried not to let anyone know. He talked through the intercom so he and the soldiers would stay awake as the highway slid beneath the gun truck's tires like a conveyor belt.

"And then Buggman," Chandler said. "Stark naked, jumps out of the lake onto the boat. It's freezing and he's standing on the edge of the pontoon, all these Fudgies staring at him, and screams, 'Look mom, no head.' It was completely insane. Still can't believe they didn't call the cops."

He lit a cigarette and laughed, listening to the static crackle in his headset.

"That was a funny story," Witkowski said after it was quiet for a long time.

"Don't lie to him," said Vogel. "There wasn't even a punch line."

Chandler slid the window open and exhaled into the fog of

heat rolling outside the vehicle. The patrol slowed as it passed a dog carcass lying stiff at the shoulder of the road, surrounded by other mongrels, long snouts and chomping teeth caked with gore as they feasted on the decaying entrails.

They drove another kilometer in silence.

"Wish I could've grown up on a beach," Gibson said. "I'd have had a boat, a sailboat. Something I could take out on the gulf all by myself."

"I lived on a lake," Chandler said. "That's not the same. The only beach we had was a thin strip of sand along parts of the shore. And a boat's expensive. Now, Buggman's dad had a real sweet Montauk, but I could never afford anything like that. I did have a canoe, though, used to paddle out on Baldwin Lake early in the morning and fish a little before it was time to meet the school bus."

"Old geezers like to fish," Vogel said.

"Blue trout," Chandler said. "I liked fishing with a simple Woolly Bugger, you can catch just about anything that swims with that little fly. It's also good for—"

"Boring," Vogel said.

Chandler tossed his cigarette out the window and looked into the desert.

"When I was old enough," he said. "I worked at Eton's grocery. Mostly made sandwiches in the deli or labeled the inventory, helped Judy bag if she was busy at the register. Old man Jim. He never did teach me how to slice the steaks and cuts of meat. And I did odd jobs for the people who owned homes on the lakes, most of them left after the season. Kept their lawns looking nice, scooped up the trash, helped install their docks when it got warm again. Also earned a little cash carving decoys, ducks, Mallards, mostly. I painted them myself and sold them from the porch, the Eton's house was behind the store, did I already tell you guys this?"

"I'm awake," Vogel said. "For fuck's sake. I'm always awake."

•

The patrol had parked on an overpass. For two days they'd driven to outposts and camps trying offload a flatbed of bottled water hauled by the convoy. No one wanted the water and they kept driving until Hurd finally radioed and told them to halt. They were going to dig a big hole in the sand and leave the water buried in the desert.

Chandler sat in his gun truck atop the bridge and glassed the long stretch of highway and sand with his binoculars. A crowd of young Iraqis had run across the desert from a settlement of walled homes. Now they squatted wearing faded robes stained in manure near the shoulder of the road, watching the soldiers.

Vogel climbed down from the turret. He went behind the vehicle and urinated and when he was done opened the trunk and closed it and returned carrying a case of bottled water. Vogel took off his helmet. He unscrewed one of the water bottles and poured it on his head, scratching his fingers through his matted hair. He smiled at the boys watching him. Then he unscrewed all the caps and emptied the case of water slowly onto the concrete one bottle at a time.

"Like that fuckers," he said. "America. We split the atom. We put men in fucking space. We even know how to remove salt from the oceans. Don't give a shit about a little water. Nope. You wait a few more years. We'll figure out how to drive our SUVs without gas. And when that happens, won't see us anymore. All you dipshit Hajjis can squat there on the road. Pick your feet and pound sand."

Vogel laughed. Gibson laughed. Witkowski snapped a photo of the boys and then he laughed, too. The boys squatted under the bright sun and picked their feet.

"Bring any more books?" Chandler said.

Vogel nodded. "Of course. I practically looted the library at Gotham."

"Then go read one," Chandler said.

"Can I hang out at Mack's truck?"

"Great idea. Please do."

"Teasdale bought a new sex doll," said Vogel. "I wanna get my swerve on."

"Do anything but what you're doing right now," Chandler said.

After he was gone, Chandler got out of his seat and pointed his toes to stretch the ache from his shins. He took an armful of cold water from the cooler in back and lobbed the bottles at the boys across the road.

The children chased the bottles sliding and spinning on the asphalt. One of the boys was missing his left arm. The curled stub of bicep visible at the end of his sleeve. He braced the water bottle between his sandaled feet and unscrewed the cap and drank. Then the boy lifted the bottle with his toes and rinsed his one hand and when he was done gave Chandler the finger.

"They do not deserve your water," Sundance said. The interpreter stood beside the open door. He wore dark goggles and gloves. His red- and white-checkered *shemagh* wrapped loosely to cover his nose and neck.

"They're little kids," Chandler said.

"They are wicked," Sundance said.

"You say that about everyone."

Sundance opened a crinkled baggie filled with *khat* and removed a pinch. He lowered his *shemagh* and jammed the dark green leaves between his gray gums and yellow teeth and covered his face again.

"Those boys," he said. "They are watching you. Counting your type of guns. How many men are in each truck. How long before you are lazy then go to sleep. Later, they will betray you to the insurgents. Heretics, all from this tribe, with one hand they take from you. The other hand sticks a knife between your ribs."

"So tell them to go away," Chandler said.

"Go away," Sundance said.

"Forget it. I'll run 'em off."

Sundance shook his head. "Shoot two of them. Then they will give you no trouble."

"You miss it?" Chandler said. "The Republican Guard. I heard you were a major, got an idea of the things you did, and I know you're not supposed to admit it to keep your job so don't if you don't want to. I really don't care and I can keep a secret."

"The old days," Sundance said. "It was nice."

"And they're over," Chandler said. "Never coming back."

"My counsel is good," Sundance said.

"I'm still not gonna shoot little kids," Chandler said.

Sundance spread his arms wide, like he was about to give a hug. He smiled beneath the *shemagh.*

"Corporal Chandler," he said. "I understand. Give me your pistol. I will shoot them for you."

That night the sky turned cold and gray and wind tore over the desert. Whipped sand hurled into the gunners, who shivered up in the turrets. The gusts rocked the gun trucks and then the clouds burst and it rained.

The patrol drove through the downpour and the highway flooded and when they couldn't see the route they parked the trucks close beneath an overpass to wait out the storm.

Gibson finished a cigarette then opened the driver's door and stepped out. He stood beside the truck, smelling the rain. He took off his body armor and helmet. He left his battle rattle on the seat and shut the door and walked to the edge of the bridge. He held out a hand to catch the falling raindrops in his palm.

"Get a load of this," Vogel said.

Gibson peeled off his uniform and boots. He left his eyeglasses on. He stepped out from under the overpass and stood naked on the road and looked up at the rain and he stood like that until he was clean.

They paid twelve dollars for half a human jawbone and a rotten earlobe from a crowd of boys who flagged down the patrol. The boys told them the remains were from a car carrying South African security contractors that'd been peeled apart by an EFP on the highway a week earlier. Mackenzie put the stinking pieces inside a biohazard bag. He radioed Hurd and asked if they could stop at the next camp. So the dead might be returned home intact. But the supply convoy was already behind schedule and the patrol drove away and as they did the boys pelted the gun trucks with stones. Mackenzie tossed the orange bag over the rail of a bridge. The bag was torn open by the stray dogs lounging underneath in the dirt. Mackenzie halted the patrol. His gun truck swung onto the cloverleaf and stopped just below the bridge. Mackenzie stood outside the door, bracing himself against the armored hatch, and shot the dogs with his carbine.

After two and a half weeks scouting for the convoys they turned back toward Camp Tucson. Now the soldiers were raggedy men with bleary eyes. The thin fabric of their fatigues had ripped at the crotch and knees. Those who could grew beards. A hole was rotted in the toe of Chandler's suede boot from the constant dripping of the leaky air vent.

The gun trucks refueled at Tallil then pushed onward. The armored frames rattled across the cracked highway as the engines lurched and coughed dark wisps of smoke. The patrol halted north of the Al Safwan cloverleaf. Chandler stepped onto the road, lit a cigarette and massaged his shins. It was quiet except for the hot breeze and the hum of the surveillance drone flying unseen overhead.

The day before another sergeant in the squad named Sullivan had developed a blood clot from sitting in the cramped vehicles and after he was evacuated Hurd took his place in the recon patrol. He waited with Mackenzie in the center lanes. "Where's Lazlo?" said Hurd.

"Wouldn't get out of the truck," Chandler told him.

Mackenzie held out his binoculars and pointed down the highway. The dead man wore a white robe and lay five hundred meters away beside the shoulder of the road. Coated in flies. No hands or feet or head. Gray tubes of intestine hung out of the stump of his neck, dangling, sprawled like tentacles onto a dark patch of sand that'd dried and hardened in the sun.

"Sir. It's a set up," Mackenzie said.

"The drone doesn't see anything," said Hurd. "There's no one else out here but us."

"First truck that drives past that thing's gonna get blown up," Mackenzie said.

"I'm not waiting," said Hurd. "It'll be dark by the time the British get here."

Chandler's gun truck closed to within two football fields of the headless body. Gibson set the parking brake and took Witkowski's camera. He put it atop the radio mount and pushed the button for video, then lit a cigarette and leaned forward, forearms resting on the steering wheel.

Vogel swung the turret around and braced himself and racked the heavy machinegun's charging handle. "Target identified," he said.

"Fire," said Chandler.

The fifty-caliber shells were armor piercing. Long bright streaks shot from the barrel. The spent brass casings dropped and rattled inside the crew compartment, scattering onto the seats and floorboards, rolling under the radio mount.

The bullets skidded off the road in front of the body. Vogel fired again. He walked the rounds in until he'd found the range. The corpse dribbled on the sand as the shells traversed along the length of the torso. The left leg peeled away from the hip and the right leg disappeared from the knee down. And then there was a quick flash that lifted the body into the air and a cone of black smoke shot out onto the highway and what was left of the corpse tumbled onto one side as the explosives buried underneath or sewn within detonated. The dead body flopped in the dust like a beanbag doll mauled by the machinegun's flaming teeth that roared across the hot and empty desert.

After it was over, they drove on towards Camp Tucson and didn't talk. The truck stank of gunpowder and burnt carbon. The patrol passed the wrecked sedan on the highway and the observation post. They passed a trio of Widow Maker trucks, then turned onto the desert trail that led to the main entrance gate.

"That story you told us," Vogel finally said. "I've been thinking about it, Corporal Chandler. And I changed my mind. 'Look mom, no head.' Now, that's some really fucking funny shit."

CHAPTER SIXTEEN

THE NEXT MORNING HE lay on his elbow beneath the poncho liner. It was quiet except for the air conditioner. Sunshine snuck inside the dark trailer through the gaps around the door. Parker's hips rocked as she pulled up her uniform pants. Then she sat on the edge of the mattress and laced up her boots.

"Let's go to breakfast," Chandler said.

"Where's my bra?"

Before the sun rose, they'd talked about all that'd happened while he was gone. A soldier in the Widow Maker company shot herself in the head and it wasn't an accident. The Ether Bunny struck again. Supply botched the chow hall's delivery manifest and for four days everyone on the camp ate sausage, white rice and bread. A soldier in Golf Company named Fazio returned from a mission and was electrocuted in the shower.

"And there's a new FOB commander," Parker said. "The old one, the Navy guy, I guess he needed something to do and decided to start running man overboard drills. Officers do it on ships. Snatch a person, hide them in a locker and then see how fast it takes the rest of crew to get accountability. But then the CO forgot about his own memorandum making all females carry a knife, and one day he jumped out between two trailers and screamed, 'Man Overboard,' and tried to grab one of the girls from the fuel point. She thought the CO was the Ether Bunny and stabbed him in the hip."

"I'm hungry," Chandler said. "Chow hall's got hash browns again."

Parker sorted through the clothes strewn on the floor. The crease between her shoulder blades visible in the dim light and Chandler leaned on his forearm to watch her. He pulled the poncho liner over the scars on his legs, thinking and waiting until she'd dressed.

"I'm gonna watch a movie tonight," he said.

"Sounds like fun."

"Maybe two movies," he said. "I'll be awake for midnight chow."

Parker cocked her floppy hat and stared. She laughed once. Then she drew her khukuri and tapped Chandler's nose with the flat side of the blade.

"Lock your door."

After she'd gone, he drew his knees in and curled under the poncho liner, a hand between his cheek and pillow. He smelled where Parker had been. He shut his eyes and tried to sleep but he was remembering what happened after she opened his trailer door and walked inside, the things she whispered for him to do with her and to her and how the experience was much more exhausting and satisfying than it'd been their first time. Being with her made him feel happy but now that she'd left, he was a little afraid. Afraid like he'd been when he woke after the surgery in Afghanistan and remembered that Reed, Tran, and Dempsey were dead.

The trailer shook and Chandler woke thinking it was an earthquake.

There was a loud crack and a long silence then the distant report of rifle and machinegun fire that was drowned out by the sirens howling across the camp.

Chandler put on his running shorts and T-shirt. He opened the trailer door and stepped into the bright sun. A whistling streaked overhead before the ground shook so violently from the explosion that he had to brace himself against the doorframe to keep from falling. The next impact was louder and felt much closer.

He listened to the sirens, heart beating fast. He backed inside and locked the trailer door. His hands shook as he fastened the zippers and buttons on his uniform.

Another shell landed on the walkway outside. The trailer was rattled hard and he thought it might fall apart as the concussion bounced him off the wall and onto his bunk.

He rolled to the floor and lay still, waiting for his ears to stop screaming. Debris fell onto the trailer roof and sounded like a rain shower and when it ceased someone next door cursed and then it was quiet except for the sirens. Dust floated in the rods of daylight that shined through the pinholes where shrapnel had pierced the thin trailer walls.

Chandler shrugged into his armored vest. He put on his helmet and buckled the chinstrap. He sat on the bed, breathing and looking at the holes in the trailer wall beside his locker. A heavy machinegun in one of the watchtowers fired a burst into the desert. After he'd sat long enough he took his carbine and assault pack and went out.

There was a jagged hole where the shell had landed on the walkway outside. The charred boards littered with splinters and pieces of gravel and steel. From the middle of the camp, smoke billowed tall and dark, twisting into the blue skies above the flat trailer roofs as Chandler jogged to the gun truck idling at the end of the block.

"Hajji got us zeroed in," Vogel said. He smiled in the gun turret wearing a T-shirt and running shorts and sneakers. He pushed a hand against his kneecaps to keep them from shaking.

"Remember? I called it," he said. "I knew this was gonna happen."

They drove to the main gate. Gravel spat from under the tires as the vehicle swerved and braked then sped down the narrow lane separating the trailer rows, dodging the runners headed to the sandbagged bunkers or to the laundry shack, where for once no one waited in line.

"They've attacked before," Chandler said.

"Not like this," Gibson told him, his knuckles tight on the steering wheel.

They passed the basketball court and saw where one of the shells had landed. It'd hit the Java Shack and punched through the roof and exploded above the register. A forklift could drive through the hole in the wall. The door was blown off and it had landed on the basketball court amid window shards and someone's suede combat boot. Flames burned inside and the Malaysian contractors tried to douse the blaze using bottles of water. Paper napkins and money tumbled over the ground. Beneath one of the basketball hoops was Batista, hunched over, scooping up singles and tens and fives blowing in the wind.

They stopped at the clearing barrels. A column of gun trucks idled near the exit queue. The soldiers strapped on the rest of their equipment and loaded their weapons. The gun truck's rear door opened. Flowers climbed in wearing his battle rattle and tapped his war club twice atop Gibson's helmet.

"Drive, Pig Pen," he said.

The column of vehicles followed them through the gate. They drove along the desert trail towards the highway and as they rounded the embankment could see the gun truck in flames near the building.

Flowers wrapped a headset over his ears and turned on the intercom.

"Mehdi Army," he said. "Really mopped the floor with your girlfriends."

Helicopters circled high above the building. Torn pieces of uniform and gauze bandages and empty saline bags blew over the desert. Spent shell casings and rifle magazines and divots where heavy machinegun bullets had impacted the sand. The burning gun truck tilted at the end of the ditch on its melted tires.

Flowers told them what'd happened. A Toyota pick-up truck stopped on the highway, not far from the wrecked sedan. Men climbed from the bed and pretended to change a tire. A second group ran across the open ground to the side of the building. The insurgents threw hand grenades in the upper windows. Three Widow Makers who survived ran out. The insurgents shot them and waited for the gun trucks on patrol. The first gun truck drove out of the ditch and was shot with a rocket-propelled grenade and the crew gunned down when they bailed out. The remaining Widow Makers flanked the insurgents and killed them with machinegun fire. The men that'd stayed with the pick-up truck had a mortar tube and launched three eighty-two millimeter shells at the camp and drove away before the attack drone could respond.

"How many dead?" Mackenzie said.

Flowers held up nine fingers. "Four Widow Makers and five bad guys."

"How in the hell?" Chandler said.

"You tell me," said Flowers. He glanced at Vogel in the gun turret. "Maybe some smart guy with all the answers told them it was OK to take a nap instead of doing their jobs."

The British demolition team arrived late in the afternoon. Their lieutenant was the officer they'd met on the highway the week before. The sores covering his arms had spread to his neck and face.

"There'll be nothing but gravel after we're finished," he told them.

"Careful in there," Chandler said.

"Explosives?"

"Blood stains. On the wall and floor," Chandler said.

The British lieutenant waved off the flies and picked his ear. "Are you having a laugh?"

"No, sir," Chandler said.

"From what I've been told, I expect to find a lot of blood on the walls and floor."

After he'd gone, Mackenzie lit a cigarette, coughing smoke as he laughed and watched as the British carried their charges and demolition gear inside.

"I wasn't trying to be funny," Chandler said.

Mackenzie shook his head. His eye twitched. "We're rolling out in the morning," he said.

"With ten days left?" Chandler said.

"Plenty of time to drive to Baghdad and back," said Mackenzie.

Chandler fingered the whistle hanging from his weapons vest and stared at the building, the smoking gun truck and the old wreckage of the sedan still on the highway.

"What's so important now?" he said. "Besides making Ingram look good?"

"The dead Hajjis," Mackenzie said. "That's our cargo. So they can be returned to their families for burial."

"How thoughtful," Chandler said.

"Cheer up. I think your buddy's coming with us."

"Stop calling him that."

The dead insurgents were in body bags lined up outside the building. Flowers paced the row then unzipped each of the bags and looked inside. After a long time Flowers swung his war club and bashed the skulls. Then he zipped up the bags and walked far into the desert, where he sat and crossed his legs on the hot sand and looked at the flames rolling from the refinery stacks on the horizon.

"No," said Witkowski. "That man's not crazy at all. He's something else."

Finally the column of vehicles drove back to camp, stopping outside near the edge of the perimeter wire to watch and wait.

A heavy clap when the British detonated the charges they'd placed in the building. The concrete walls crumbled one at a time and then the roof dropped into the rubble and the building was swallowed in a cloud of gray dust as hunks of concrete splashed into the soft sand and then the desert was quiet again.

The implosion swept a shockwave over the desert and most of the soldiers cheered except for Vogel. He stood in the gun turret, leaning against the cupola with his arms crossed. He didn't talk until they'd returned to camp.

There was a convoy briefing that night and afterward Chandler walked to the lower enlisted neighborhood. Deserted walkways and quiet except for the groan of the generators. He'd planned to check on the soldiers then pack his gear and take a shower. He didn't know if Parker had been killed or wounded during the shelling and he wanted to be ready in case she visited him later.

Gibson and Witkowski sat on the steps outside the trailer with a case of bottled water. They watched a fire burning in a steel drum on the gravel nearby. Book pages twirled out of the orange flames and landed on the wood planks, glowing faint in the darkness before they curled into ash.

"Vogel's library," said Gibson. "He torched it all."

"Where's he at now?" Chandler said.

"Lifting weights," said Witkowski.

"He was standing out here alone," Gibson said. "Tore up his books and burned 'em one page at a time."

Chandler lit a cigarette. The flames inside the barrel hissed like a funeral pyre licked by the breeze. He thought about Vogel and what they'd talked about that last night in the observation post.

"Is he armed?" he said.

Witkowski nodded. "But he left his ammo. So we wouldn't worry and try to find him."

"He knew those girls," Chandler said.

"From the party," said Witkowski.

A helicopter flew overhead and landed on the pad outside the camp aid station. Chandler waited until it'd flown away. "And he told them what to expect out in the building," he said.

Gibson nodded. "Called it a big joke. Guess now he's sad, probably feels real guilty."

Chandler tossed his cigarette into the barrel.

"No. That's not what he's upset about."

CHAPTER SEVENTEEN

THE PATROL DROVE TO Baghdad and escorted the convoy into the Green Zone. The dead insurgents were delivered to one of the morgues and after staying three days they left for Camp Tucson. They rolled slowly along the highway south of Tallil under a gray sky, through hundred and thirty-five degree heat.

Chandler smoked, exhaling through the open window. He watched the sand and rocks and trash at the roadside. Through his side mirror, the gun trucks and the armored Freightliner in the main convoy followed far in the distance.

He was hot and bored and he thought about whether to enroll in college in the fall or skip a semester. About the letter Judy Eton had written and the places where he might scatter Jim's ashes. And about Parker, how she didn't visit the night before he'd left, if he'd done something wrong or their relationship was a one off and she'd simply moved on. He now knew she hadn't been killed in the attack on the camp but didn't know if she was among the wounded. He wanted to see her again.

"First sergeant bought a Persian rug," Gibson said. "He had me drive him to the main PX over on Gotham. Sat in the Hajji shop forty-five minutes, looking through a magnifying glass, before he found the one he wanted."

"Loony fucker," said Vogel. "It's his last chance to buy something. He didn't have to let Batista come, too. Guess what Shorty wasted his pay on: Three custom-tailored suits. Dumbass."

They drove and listened to the sounds in the gun truck and

tried to ignore the dense heat.

Chandler swallowed his painkillers and massaged the ache in his shins, holding his face close to the open window. In the desert outside, the clouds had parted and thin rays of sunshine painted the sand. The patrol neared one of the overpasses. On the left, where the crossroad passed beneath the bridge, was a long house and smaller walled homes. There was static on the radio and Gibson humming "Big Rock Candy Mountain" through the intercom.

The gun truck's engine growled. A baritone whine as the tires rolled over cracks in the highway. Chandler leaned into the windshield, looking for the children who on an earlier trip had lurked in the roadside ditch to throw rocks at the passing vehicles. But he saw no one, only Hurd's gun truck, the red stop sign on the spare tire and the gunner up in the turret, nodding his head, listening to his iPod.

Chandler thought about Afghanistan and the calm before the ambush in the wheat field. His hand shook as he sipped coffee from his thermos. He told himself they had crossed this bridge many times before and there was no reason to be afraid.

The vehicles drove over the bridge and the bomb exploded in the median.

Hurd's gun truck swerved then was swallowed in the cloud of dark smoke and grit that washed over the road. There was a loud bang. Chandler braced his hands against the dash as the shockwave shook his truck. Cracks appeared in the windshield. The truck braked and cold coffee spilled on his thighs when the seatbelt locked up and slammed him against the seat cushion.

The patrol stopped. It was quiet except for the sound of the gravel hitting the hood of Chandler's gun truck. He relaxed his grip on the dash and inhaled, smelled the cordite coughed out by the bomb. The smoke cleared and he saw Hurd's truck appear like a parlor trick prestige. That's when the insurgents who waited in the long house opened fire.

The tracers were green and red. The bullets raked the driver's side of Hurd's gun truck, and then beside it was a firecracker flash where the rocket-propelled grenade hit. The firing increased when the insurgents found the range. Hurd's gun truck sagged. The bullets tore into the tires and chiseled chips of plastic off the trunk and hood. A trail of vapor from the second rocket-propelled grenade streaked from the roof of the house. The rocket exploded on the armored strip between the gun cupola and the doors, forty or fifty meters away.

Now the noise of shots and explosions was louder and Chandler heard pings, like marbles or hail, hitting his truck. The insurgents had zeroed in. A bullet entered through the rear window. Witkowski groaned when his cheek was peppered with shards of flying glass. The spent bullet jacket tumbled wild inside the steel cab until it hit Chandler's thermos and coffee exploded onto the windshield.

"Waste 'em," Chandler said.

Vogel spun the hand crank and swung the gun turret and aimed at the long house. There was a rumble and a pair of shell casings and links from his heavy machinegun fell inside the crew compartment. Then there was the metallic pong from a bullet ricocheting off the turret shield.

Vogel slumped into the cab. His head flopped face up in Chandler's lap.

He'd been shot in the helmet. Charred fabric looped the hole in the helmet cover next to the mount for his night-vision goggles. Inside the hole, a bullet jacket nestled between the flecks of tan Kevlar fibers. Vogel's protective eyeglasses fell off and Gibson screamed when he saw the blank eyes staring up at him. But there was no blood. Chandler heard Vogel breathing through the nose and flicked an index finger against his eyeball.

"Waffles with toasted cheese and jelly," Vogel said. Then he was unconscious again.

The insurgents kept shooting.

Hurd opened the passenger door when his gun truck started

to burn. He stepped onto the road, confused, then sunk to his knees and vomited. Smoke thickened from the gun turret and the open door. The gunner fell out through the haze of smoke with an arm on fire. He lay in the pool of Hurd's vomit and smacked at the flames. The driver crawled out the door and shoved him into the roadside ditch. He rolled the gunner in the sand until the arm stopped burning then he hugged him close and began to sob.

Sundance had exited on the wrong side. He was trapped between the vehicle and the kill zone. He lay on the highway and screamed. The bullets screamed louder. Then he got up and ran towards the long house, waving his red- and white-checkered shemagh. He made it a few strides and was shot in the shoulder. He spun, stumbling and running, waving his scarf and yelling until he was shot through the stomach. He made a face and folded up on the highway. Sundance didn't move after that but the insurgents kept shooting him anyway.

"Jesus Christ," Chandler said. He pulled the door latch and pushed. He was leaving, getting out of the gun truck and walking away. You're done, Chandler told himself. These fools signed up for a fight and now they're in one and it's a jam and it's got nothing to do with you. Go. Get out before you get chopped like Reed and Dempsey and Tran or really nailed again. Not brave. Not a hero. Not smart enough to know when you're in over your head. You can fix that. You owe these people nothing. No more. Leaving now.

He lifted Vogel's head and unbuckled the seatbelt. His hands grasped the outer edges of the door hatch. He pushed off the way he'd been taught in airborne school. Chandler tucked in his arms and chin and prepared to roll once he hit the highway. He shut his eyes and felt himself fall forward and then a hard tug.

Chandler opened his eyes. He hung half outside the door, suspended from the gun truck a few inches above the ground. The whistle fastened to his ammunition vest had snagged on the door latch. He grabbed it, breathing hard as he jerked and twisted the paracord in his fists. He couldn't break free. Like a trout hooked on the line and for a moment he thought he heard the sound of the reel spinning. A bullet skipped off the asphalt near his head. Chandler pulled again then reached for the knife in his calf pocket. He pushed the button and snapped the switchblade open. He slashed the whistle's lanyard and fell onto the highway.

Chandler lay on the road. He listened to the shooting. Finally he rose and knelt by the open door to the truck. His carbine was on the seat. His heart beat fast against the plate in his body armor.

"Get out," he said. "Get out of the truck and fight."

Vogel was heavy and limp and they had to kick and heave his body out of the door. They dragged him to the ditch. Witkowski wiped at the blood on his face. Then he unfolded the automatic rifle's bipod and began shooting at the long house, which Chandler guessed was about two football fields away. He peered over top of the ditch. The insurgents shot from the windows. On the roof stood a walled gazebo and through the gap in the wall there was the long thin launch tube and the puff of back-blast when another rocket-propelled grenade careened overhead and boomed behind them in the desert.

He told the soldiers to keep shooting.

He ran along the top of the ditch. He touched the side to keep from sliding on the loose sand. He felt the whoosh of large insects flying above and past his head and remembered the first time he'd heard that sound and tried to ignore it. He reached the third gun truck. Mackenzie had gotten out and knelt behind the front tire. He had a grin and his eye had stopped twitching.

"Relax. You're still alive," Mackenzie said. "We'll get out of this. First, I need you to—"

Mackenzie was shot in the throat. His body went stiff and the smile erased from his lips. He clasped the side of his neck and blood oozed from between his fingers as he toppled forward.

"Gelp," he said.

He slumped on top of Chandler. Thrashing in a tantrum like a baby pulled from his mother's embrace. The blood warm on Chandler's pants and sleeves as he slid out from beneath Mackenzie.

Chandler left him on the dirt beside the tire, grabbing his throat, legs flailing. He didn't want to look at the sergeant, so he ran.

The last gun truck had stopped on the overpass. The gunner was shooting and links from the belt bounced off Chandler's helmet as he tried to open the passenger door. It was locked from inside. He pounded the heel of his hand on the glass and yelled until the window opened a crack.

"What do you want?" Lazlo said.

"Mack's down. Hurd's down," Chandler said.

"This is so fucked."

"You're next in the chain of command."

Lazlo blinked. "I'm calling for help."

Chandler pounded on the window glass. "We can't stay here. We'll get picked off and any help from the convoy or gunships won't get here in time."

"Secure the scene," Lazlo said.

"We need to maneuver," Chandler said.

"I'll radio first sergeant." Lazlo slammed the window shut and crouched low under the dashboard.

Chandler got on his knees and lit a cigarette, shaking and breathing. He looked at the long house. The walled homes nearby. At the bridge and the trucks in the main convoy that'd stopped several kilometers back on the highway.

He pounded on the window until it opened.

"Your gunner," he told Lazlo. "Have him shoot at the windows. Don't worry about that thing on the roof. Shift fire when you see me come out from under the bridge."

"The hell you going?" Lazlo said.

"To make a decision." Chandler flicked his cigarette off the overpass and ran.

He skirted the ditch until he'd returned to the third gun truck. The medic had gotten out and his knees were pinned on Mackenzie's arms to hold them still while he bandaged the hole in the sergeant's throat.

Chandler opened the back door. He grabbed the anti-tank rocket and slung it across his back. He motioned for the driver to crawl out and told him to take Mackenzie's grenade launcher and then pointed out where he wanted him to lob smoke and fragmentation grenades.

Chandler's legs hurt as he ran through the hum of large insects.

The insurgents kept shooting at the vehicles and the soldiers in the ditch. On the road lay sheets of armor plate and a chunk of machinegun barrel. A burnt patch marred where the rocket-propelled grenade had struck the turret of Chandler's gun truck. Gibson and Witkowski had moved the wounded away from the flames consuming Hurd's vehicle. Chandler felt the heat from where they now lay amid the spent brass casings and links, alternating to rise from the ditch and engage the insurgents in the house.

The wounded lay at the bottom of the ditch. Vogel was still unconscious. Hurd gagged from smoke inhalation. His driver had a concussion and the gunner a deep open gash where the sleeve was melted to his broken arm.

Chandler swung the rocket launcher onto his shoulder. He raised the sights and pulled the safety pin and cocked it so the launcher was ready to fire. "Back-blast area clear."

Witkowski reloaded the ammunition belt. Then he braced the automatic rifle in his armpit and held the twin pistol grips as he fired. The lubricant in the feed tray was hot. A white fog spat from the ejection port and the end of the short barrel.

After he'd fired three bursts, Chandler stood up from the ditch with the launch tube and pressed the forward safety. There was loud boom as the anti-tank rocket fired and a heavy thud when it hit the gazebo atop the long house.

The three of them slid down the embankment and ran beneath the overpass. The shooting echoed loud among the pillars. They ran out from under the bridge and hugged the embankment until they'd reached the long house. They pressed against the wall in a file and walked slowly to the far corner.

Smoke hovered on the roof above but the shooting from inside had stopped. Machinegun fire from the gun trucks crackled over the desert and along the empty street where Chandler waited next to a billboard for Iraqna cell phones. He peeked around the corner into an alley that separated the long house from a smaller home. At the opposite end of the alley, a dusty Mercedes sedan idled and behind the steering wheel sat a man with his face veiled by a shemagh.

Chandler raised his carbine. He aimed through the open driver's window. He took a breath and let it out halfway, sighting between the man's eyebrows.

He squeezed the trigger.

The driver jerked upright then laid his forehead on the steering wheel. Chandler continued shooting, into the side door and windshield. He kept shooting as he crossed the alley to the edge of the small house, aiming at the tires and the hood ornament and the radiator. He reloaded the magazine and as he did a narrow door opened on the backside of the long house. A short man clothed in a black hood and a dishdasha entered the alley. He held a rifle and a hand grenade.

Gibson leveled his carbine cut the man down as he started to run towards the Mercedes.

Then more men came out through the narrow door one at a time and they made a break across the alley, headed for the sedan or the smaller home. Chandler, Gibson and Witkowski shot them but they ran very fast and at least four escaped through a doorway on the other side.

Now there were five dead stretching across the alley. A sixth slumped in the Mercedes. All clad in dark dishdashas or Nike tracksuits, Reebok high tops or leather boots, faces wrapped in checkered shemaghs, the magazines for their Steyr and Galil and Kalashnikov rifles tucked in canvas chest harnesses. One of the insurgents wore a pair of Ray-Bans.

"These guys are not Mehdi Army," Witkowski said.

The soldiers reloaded and shot the dead insurgents again.

Chandler spat onto the dirt. He was angry. Not because the patrol was ambushed. This was a war and he understood that. He was angry because after he fell out of his gun truck he'd stopped thinking of anyone in his team or squad as men or as soldiers. He'd thought of them as resources.

These insurgents were different, Chandler thought. Not militia. Well equipped and their attack was lethal. But they'd also been colossally stupid. He'd studied the manuals on tactics and played enough *Call of Duty* with Buggman to realize they'd left their flank unsecured then were outmaneuvered and surprised in the alley. The man who Gibson had shot probably was the leader and planned to escape in the Mercedes. The others would retreat to the small home and wait for reinforcements from the convoy to arrive before they attacked again.

Chandler pushed a finger to his lips. He replaced the magazine in his carbine and turned the selector switch so it'd fire three bullets when he pulled the trigger.

They stacked up at the door to the smaller house and went inside. The floor tiles smooth and slick as they stepped over a pile of leather sandals and children's slippers. Bright red droplets led to a small kitchen. Staircase cracks in the mud walls. An oil lamp hung in one corner and on the wall table was a hot plate stove and plastic tubs filled with brass kettles and pans.

A hallway led into the center of the house. Chandler knelt and looked around the corner. The light was dim and the rug on the floor smelled of feet and feces. No one was in the narrow passage or visible in the dark doorway at the opposite end.

Witkowski gripped the twin pistol grips to his automatic rifle. He thumbed off the safety and turned the corner. He spun and ran back when three rifle shots flashed and thundered from the doorway.

"*Allahu Akbar*."

"Pieces of shit," Witkowski said.

They're bunkered in and the hallway acts like a funnel, Chandler thought. He turned when someone tugged his sleeve. It was Gibson, holding the fragmentation grenade he'd shown Chandler that last night in the observation post.

"Never gave it back to Shorty," he told him.

Chandler nodded. "Roll it down there," he said.

"You do it."

"This is why you came over here," Chandler said. "Do it now. Pretend you're bowling."

Gibson licked his lips and leaned his carbine on the wall. He peeled off the electrical tape wrapped around the spoon and safety pin. He crouched at the corner with the grenade tight in his chest. He pulled the pin and lobbed it down the hallway without looking then stuck his fingers in his ears. A ping and a hiss as the spoon popped off then the clang of bouncing steel. The grenade exploded and the hallway filled with black smoke and dust.

"*Allahu Akbar.*"

Two insurgents charged out of the cloud into the kitchen. Chandler fired a burst from his carbine as he was tackled and slid on his back across the tiled floor.

He batted at the hand on his throat. Blur of mad brown eyes and a curly stub of beard and snapping teeth. Stink of old sweat and bad breath. He was kneed in the groin and punched in the jaw. Fingers squeezed his windpipe.

Chandler tried to punch and kick back but he was tired. Then he grabbed a handful of the man's sleeve and thrust his hips and rolled on the tiles until the weight of his body armor and ammunition leveraged him on top. He pushed his knee into the man's chest and yanked his ear and a wad of wet hair. He butted the man in the face with the brim of his helmet. Then he put his thumbs against the man's eyes and pushed down hard. He pushed with his thumbs, slamming the man's head against the floor, pounding and pushing until finally the man stopped struggling and the blood oozed hot and thick onto the tile.

Gibson sat against the wall. He'd seized the other insurgent from behind and choked him with his forearms. The insurgent twisted but couldn't break free. Witkowski knelt in front with his knife, working the blade like a sewing machine needle, piercing the ribs and stomach.

When it was over they stood in the kitchen with their hands on their kneecaps, breathing and listening at the entrance to the hallway.

"*Allah.*"

Gibson pinched his nose and squeezed out a cord of blood. "Can't be more than two left."

Chandler coughed. His hands shook while he rolled the dead insurgents. He felt in the pockets of their dishdashas and equipment belts. He was searching for more grenades. He didn't know how many were still in the bunker at the end of the hall. He thought about retreating out of the kitchen and looking for a staircase to the roof and attacking from the high ground.

He found a toy rubber airplane in the pocket of the man he'd killed.

"Like the prize from a Happy Meal," Witkowski said.

Chandler turned the rubber airplane in his hands, thinking. There was no cockpit. The hull was bent and it'd been hand-painted blue with tiny yellow flowers and red stripes on the wings.

"Listen," Gibson said. "The gun trucks. They stopped shooting."

Chandler nodded. A child's toy, he told himself, a little airplane without a pilot that'd been painted with flowers. He thought about that. Then he swallowed and stood up and shoved Gibson and Witkowski towards the door.

"The drone," he said. "Jesus Christ. Run."

CHAPTER EIGHTEEN

The strike drone launched a missile at the small house. It entered through a window and exploded in the common room. A section of the roof and outer wall collapsed. It was quiet after the debris and dust settled.

Chandler smoked in the heat, leaning against the side of the outbuilding where they'd run to hide. Witkowski sat drinking water in the dirt. He kept still while Gibson plucked the shards of glass from his cheek with a pair of Leatherman pliers.

"That Hajji broke my nose," Gibson said. His voice was different now that he'd plugged his bloody nostrils with cigarette butts.

Blackhawks landed on the highway to pick up the wounded and the dead. It was a long time before gun trucks from the convoy arrived with an assault force to clear the buildings. A surveillance drone was on station and flew somewhere in the clouds, the faint sound of its motor drowned out by the Apache gunships circling above.

Flowers waited in the alley. He nudged the dead insurgents with his boot and took off their shemaghs. He gripped his war club and twisted their noses hard and when he was certain they were dead, leaned in close to examine them.

"Al Qaeda," Flowers said. "We got a Syrian. Two Chechnyans. Definitely an Iraqi. I'm gonna guess and say this one's Bosnian. Somebody dialed 1-800-Henchmen. Really put together a mixed bag."

"Don't sound surprised," Chandler said.

"And neither should you," Flowers said. "How else do you think a drone mission ended up assigned to this sleepy sector? The CIA hoards these birds like a squirrel does nuts. But these dead fucks here, the spooks have been looking to bag them for a long, long time."

"And we were the bait," Chandler said. "Thanks for telling us."

Flowers frowned and cocked his head.

"Only way to drop the hammer on these evil idiots was to let them hit us first," he said.

Chandler spat. "Woolly Bugger."

"What?" Flowers said.

"Never mind."

Chandler leaned against the hood of a gun truck. There was grape soda in the cooler and after he drank one he lit a cigarette. He let what'd happened sink in and felt ill, watching as Batista set his carbine on top of the Mercedes then lift the dead driver's head off the steering wheel as he looked inside.

"We haven't searched them yet," Chandler told him.

"Dibs on this guy's Omega," said Batista.

"Watch out. Booby traps."

"Damn," Batista said. "Whoever plugged this Hajji made one hell of a shot."

Chandler drew on the cigarette and blew smoke out of his nose. He saw his aviator's gloves stained and stiff with dried blood. He took them off and scrubbed his bare hands with sand.

Flowers watched him and laughed.

"Talked to operations," he said. "Captain Ingram's very happy. Should've heard all the cheering in the background. Those Fobbits riding desks act like they put a man on the moon."

"That airstrike almost got us killed," Chandler said.

"The drone has a camera," Flowers said. "The controllers waited until you'd left. You'd have known what was happening if you'd brought a radio. But you were too busy playing hero."

"What if there were civilians inside?"

"Was there?"

Chandler smoked his cigarette.

Flowers stared at him and smiled. Then he swept his war club over the insurgents lying dead in the alley. "Which one's the honcho?" he said.

"Got your camera?" said Gibson.

"Left it in the truck," Witkowski said.

Flowers shrugged. He grabbed one of the dead by the hair and raised the club and he was about to bring it down when the grenade exploded inside the Mercedes.

Chandler ducked behind the gun truck when he heard the pop. He waited, then looked over the hood as the dark smoke cleared. Batista lay on his stomach beside the car door. He held the driver's severed arm with the expensive watch on its wrist and he lay very still.

Flowers turned Batista over. There was a large blackened hole where the mouth and nose should've been. Flowers flung his war club on the sand. He knelt and spoke into Batista's ear but the noise of the helicopters was too loud and no one could hear him.

They stayed on the highway overnight, waiting for the British demolition team to check the houses and the dead insurgents. For the Iraqi police to remove the bodies and for wreckers to tow the damaged gun trucks back to Camp Tucson.

Smell of gunpowder and burnt hair and diesel fuel. A gang of Iraqi kids wearing rags squatted along the embankment at the end of the bridge. They stayed until sunset, to collect the spent brass casings and whatever else might be left over from the ambush. But the soldiers didn't leave so the children walked back to their homes in the desert.

Chandler traversed the road in the darkness. He shined his flashlight, sweeping the bright cone over the battleground. He searched for Sergeant Reed's whistle, which he'd cut loose while trying to get out of his vehicle. He couldn't find it. He'd carried it so long and although he knew the whistle was lost he looked for it anyway. After a long time he became tired and turned off the light and lay across the hood of Mackenzie's gun truck. He removed his helmet and scratched his head and smoked, looking at the night sky, thinking.

The wounded were flown to Camp Tucson. Vogel woke up in the aid station and was returned to duty. Hurd and his driver and gunner were transferred to Kuwait and booked on a medical flight to Germany.

Another helicopter ferried Mackenzie, Batista and Sundance to the morgue in Baghdad.

"This means Lazlo's our squad leader now," said Witkowski.

"I don't work for that asshole," Gibson said. He smiled and lit Chandler another cigarette.

The convoy returned to Camp Tucson in the morning. The sun was hot and bright and the air bore a slight wind as the vehicles were refueled and parked in the motor pool.

Gibson and Witkowski went to the aid station. They needed to have their wounds treated and documented in their medical records to receive Purple Hearts. Chandler was hungry but the chow hall was closed until lunchtime. He helped the remaining soldiers download the gun trucks then shouldered his gear.

"Where you going?" Lazlo said.

Chandler shrugged. "Somewhere."

"We gotta write statements," Lazlo said.

Chandler nodded and lit a cigarette.

"Got something for you," Lazlo said. He held out the AK-47 bayonet he'd taken from the Bedouin. Chandler pulled it from the scabbard. A hunk of ash from the cigarette in his mouth fell and rolled off the blade as he ran his thumb along the edge.

"I took charge," Lazlo said. "Yesterday on the highway. I knew what I was doing."

"We're good," said Chandler.

"I was delegating authority," Lazlo said.

"Then write that in your report," said Chandler. He sheathed the bayonet and put it in his assault pack.

"And we're OK?" Lazlo said.

"Why wouldn't we be?" He reached in his pocket. He tossed Lazlo the toy airplane found on the man he'd beaten to death.

"Fuck is this supposed to be?" Lazlo said.

"A souvenir. You promised your boys," Chandler told him.

He was laughing after he'd left the motor pool and walked along the gravel road to the main section of camp. Laughing because he'd shipped to Iraq feeling guilty and afraid of being called afraid. Then what he'd been most afraid of happening had happened. He was laughing because this time the outcome was different than it'd been in Afghanistan. And even though people had died, this time it didn't sting as much. He knew he didn't want to be in the Army. Or stationed on Camp Tucson. But he was thinking about Parker and he laughed because now he'd be leaving very soon and had found someone who'd given him a reason to stay.

Now that's funny, Chandler thought.

He was still laughing when he arrived at Parker's communications shop. He set his equipment on the bench outside the door and went inside, smiling.

Ravi spun in the torn leather chair. The lights turned low and incense burned thick and sweet in the forty-millimeter casing on the desk. Ravi stopped spinning and removed his headphones when the door opened. He opened his mouth and stared at Chandler, at his red eyes and torn fatigues stained with grime and sweat and the blood of two men.

"Problem with your radio?" he said.

"Looking for Sergeant Parker," Chandler said.

"She's gone," said Ravi.

"I can wait," Chandler said. He sat on a high chair beside the wooden shelves.

"You'll be waiting a long time," said Ravi.

Chandler stopped smiling. "Where is she?"

"Told you. She's gone."

"What do you mean, gone?"

"Gone home. Emergency leave."

Chandler put a cigarette in his mouth. He started to light up but stopped then rolled it in his fingers. "Who died?"

Ravi shook his head. "Got sick. Her husband. Had a stroke."

"Her husband."

"A staff sergeant," Ravi said. "Recruiter stationed at Fort Sill. Now he's a cripple. She's gotta take care of this poor dude. And little Tasha."

"That's her daughter?" Chandler said.

"Lhasa Apso," Ravi told him.

Chandler lit his cigarette. He let the smoke roll in his lungs then exhaled very slow.

"Do you want some water?" Ravi said.

"What's that?" said Chandler.

"Water. Would you like a bottle of water?"

"No, thank you."

"Water's good stuff. You'll die without it."

Chandler hopped off the chair and limped across the shop to the desk. He snuffed out his cigarette in the forty-millimeter casing and lit another. "OK if I smoke in here?"

Ravi nodded. He rocked in his seat and watched Chandler climb back onto the high chair and smoke.

"Is it cold?" Chandler said after a long time.

"Huh?" said Ravi.

"The water. I think I'd like some cold water now."

He left the shop, smoking as he walked slowly across the camp. He thought about Parker and if she would try to contact him and or if he should and if she planned to tell her husband and if he'd been the only man, or woman, she'd been with during her tour. He flicked the butt on the ground. He lit another. Sweating. He walked to the Java Shack but it'd been razed and all that was left was a concrete slab. Then he walked on the packed gravel road, under the watchtowers alongside the earth embankment. Past the helicopter landing pad and the abandoned detention facility, towards the garbage dump.

Fire and black smoke belched from the burn pit. A group of Smurfs in blue jumpsuits melted the trash they'd collected from around the camp. The Iraqi workers stood in the heat and smell of burning plastic water bottles filled with urine, blinking as Chandler approached holding the AK-47 bayonet.

He asked the workers if they'd seen the Bedouin. If any of them knew when the young man might return. The men shook their heads and blinked and went back to work. He watched them shovel in the plastic bags of refuse and stoke the fires, thinking.

Finally he chucked the bayonet into the fire. He smoked a cigarette and watched the bayonet disappear as more garbage was piled on. Then he limped back to his trailer under the hot summer sun.

Nighttime and there was a fog in Baghdad. The blue landing lights on the airstrip shone through the haze. Outside the terminal, the soldiers hunched on a low wall of sandbags, watching mortar shells explode far in the distance, throwing sparks onto the tarmac.

"Drank a lot of Coors Banquet after my first tour," Chandler told them. "And this time, I'm gonna drink even more. In a month or two, you may decide to go back to work or to school. But if you do it won't be because you want to. People, man, they won't shut up. Watch. They'll keep asking what you're going to do now that you're back home. Compared to life downrange, I think it might be impossible to find anything as interesting."

He lit a cigarette and held it low, cupped in his hands. He

turned to the three soldiers who sat beside him staring at the ground, waving off the flies.

"The leaves and grass," Chandler went on. "It'll seem greener than green. And the air won't smell like dog crap. At the airport, don't be surprised if there's a crowd of old dudes from the local USO, clapping and wanting to shake your hand. That's nice. Means a lot. But after the long flight, all you'll really want to do is find the closest latrine and take a leak."

A flare launched from a nearby guard tower lit behind them in the fog. Their shadows stretched long across the gravel ramp as the flare rocked under its parachute and fell among the neighborhood of houses outside the perimeter wall.

A pair of C-130 cargo planes taxied down the runway. The propellers turned as the planes rolled towards the hangar. The ground shook hard as another shell exploded unseen in the fog.

Vogel spat. "Fucking Hajjis better not blow up my freedom bird."

After a while they left Chandler alone on the sandbags. He drank the espresso Witkowski had brought him. He watched the shelling and the long red tracer bullets arcing into the dark sky far off above the city. Finally he felt a connection to the soldiers, what he'd lost and had searched for since Afghanistan. He had thought that would make him happy, and it did, but mostly he felt sad because now they were leaving and he knew, like Parker, they would never be together again.

When the shelling had stopped there was a company formation outside the terminal. The soldiers slouched in the ranks and Ingram pinned their combat badges and medals and campaign ribbons to their uniforms. Afterward the soldiers mingled and scratched themselves in the dim light, waiting until it was time to load the two planes now parked at the end of the ramp.

Chandler returned to the sandbagged wall and sat. He unclasped the campaign medal the commander had pinned to his uniform. The polyester ribbon was colored with red and green and white and black and brown stripes. A bronze disk hung from the ribbon. On the obverse was a map of Iraq and palm fronds, the other side a statue and crossed swords. It weighed nothing as he held it his hand.

Flowers walked up on him quietly in the dark. He stood behind the wall, watching. "A soldier will fight long and hard for a piece of colored ribbon," he finally said.

"Bit," said Chandler.

"Bit of what?" Flowers said.

"Bit of colored ribbon," said Chandler. "The translation. That's what Napoleon meant."

"You know, young corporal, but you don't understand."

Flowers stepped over the sandbags and sat beside Chandler. "Get what you came for?" he said.

Chandler shrugged. "Ask me in twenty years if it was worth it."

"Why the sad face?" Flowers said.

"Lazlo," Chandler said. "He got a Bronze Star. For valor. How'd you pull that off?"

Flowers turned to where Lazlo stood alone in the dark against the wall of the terminal. He laughed.

"A minor celebrity," he said. "He'll get his picture in the newspaper. Ride on a parade float. Civilians love to see a real war hero eating those free breadsticks at Olive Garden. Makes everyone in the states wish they'd been a part of this patriotic adventure."

"It's a sham," Chandler said. "These medals won't even buy you a bus ride. Back home the people don't even know what they mean. Jesus Christ. Maybe it's better if they don't."

Flowers balanced his elbows on his knees and wrung his hands.

"Hear the good news?" he said. "I've signed on for another deployment. Time for me to pay another visit to Afghanistan."

"Good for you," Chandler said. "Who's the lucky outfit?"

"A National Guard brigade based out of Oregon," Flowers said. "They've got a special mission, too. Ever hear of a Provincial Reconstruction Team? The eastern provinces, snow on those mountains along the Pakistani border. Gorgeous in wintertime."

Chandler shook his head. "I'll send you a care package."

"All I have to do is make a phone call," Flowers said. "I can have you back downrange in five months. I'll keep an eye on you and that way you can give yourself another go. To really set things right. It'll be like going home."

Chandler pulled a sick-call slip from his cargo pocket and held out it for Flowers to see.

"Decided to take your advice," he said. "Went to see the medics. Got a no battle rattle, no running profile. And after I out process stateside, I'll never wear a uniform again. Safe to say I'm done with this insanity."

Flowers leaned over and picked a cigarette but off the ground and rolled it in his palm.

"You never served in peacetime," he said. "Training for a battle that never happens. It's like being a librarian in a world without books. Trust me, that's insanity."

"Talk to Vogel," Chandler said. "Maybe he'll go to Afghanistan with you."

"Civilian world. It's a dead end. Man knows where he stands here. Where he belongs." Flowers sucked his teeth and stared at the planes and the end of the ramp.

Then he told Chandler what happened a few weeks after he was wounded in Afghanistan. The platoon escorted a colonel to a nearby village for a *shura*. Outside with the security cordon, one of the farmers who lived in the village approached and asked the paratroopers why they were there, in his country. Flowers said he told the farmer they'd come so someday their sons wouldn't have to fight each other. After the farmer thought about that he puffed out his chest and told them that his wives had given him many sons.

"That stuck with me," Flowers said. "How do you defeat an enemy who thinks like that? See, in a way, you're right, Chandler. We've been sent to execute a mission with no end game. A sham. Once a solider figures that out, what they're up against, morale is gone, unless someone dangles the carrot from the stick. That's my specialty. How I know I belong in this war."

Chandler stepped on his cigarette and lit another. "And when it's over?"

"We'll never leave," Flowers said. "The Army might pack it up and roll out in a few years, but America? We're not going anywhere. Not all the way."

Flowers snorted and pointed at the row of concrete blast walls beside the terminal. He told Chandler how each barricade cost nine thousand dollars and there was a factory on the other side of the base that couldn't make them fast enough. Same story over at the bottled water plant. That it didn't matter if soldiers couldn't protect convoys or prevent the camps from being attacked or even catch the Ether Bunny. That billions of dollars would keep getting funneled into Iraq and Afghanistan by idiots in an air-conditioned office in Washington who think spending money will solve a problem that can't be solved with money. He told Chandler that the only thing those kinds of people did know was that the country that wins in Iraq, wins anywhere. Idiots, like Ingram, dressed in suits, and who like to make money and make decisions. Flowers went on. He went on about how he didn't understand why civilians and the press at home even complained about the war except maybe because they were cowards and that's about when Chandler stopped listening. He stopped listening because he realized this was a lecture Flowers had rehearsed, a speech he had been waiting to make for a very long time.

"First sergeant," Chandler said.

"Don't interrupt me," said Flowers.

"I've changed my mind."

"Almost at the good part. Wait for it."

"You are crazy."

Flowers looked at him with his narrow eyes. Then he gently squeezed Chandler's knee and laughed.

"Keep telling yourself that. Buddy."

An hour later the soldiers put on their helmets and body armor, shouldered their assault packs then stood in a long file outside the terminal.

The aircrews lowered the ramps and the troop seats. On each aisle was a box of earplugs and another with airsickness bags. The propellers began to turn and the soldiers shuffled up the ramp.

"Congratulations. Heard they're finally gonna promote you to sergeant," Chandler said.

"Big deal," said Vogel.

"You pulled it off," Chandler told him. "Combat veteran. Purple Heart. Exactly what you wanted."

Vogel squinted against the warm propeller wash that watered his eyes.

"Kidding me?" he said. "I fired two shots in combat. Then I got knocked out stone cold. What a fucking joke."

The propellers spun faster and the soldiers shuffled up the ramp.

Chandler buckled himself into the seat near the jump door. He leaned back into the netting that divided the cargo hold. The soldiers cheered. They laughed and stomped on the metal floor. Their fists pounded each other's helmets. They hugged whoever sat beside them. They screamed and they were beyond happy.

The celebration stopped when a van pulled up to the plane and a steel crate was wheeled out and loaded into the cargo hold. The crate was a heavy steel rectangle. Draped over top and secured tight at the corners was an American flag.

The soldiers watched and didn't talk as the aircrew strapped the coffin to the floor. Then the ramp raised and the cargo hold closed and the engines revved. The plane wobbled as it began to taxi down the runway.

Gibson jerked his chin at the coffin. "That what I think it is?"

Witkowski nodded. He snapped a photo with the new camera he'd bought at the PX.

"That's a helluva thing," Gibson said.

The engines roared as the plane accelerated. Chandler felt himself pulled towards the tail section. He grasped the netting to keep from sliding on the seat. The plane vaulted into sky. The nose swung straight up into the fog and the clouds and climbed fast to avoid being struck by anti-aircraft fire.

The plane shook. The coffin rattled loud against the metal floorboards. Chandler listened to the sound and he wanted a cigarette. He knew there was a person lying in the coffin and that person wasn't a person anymore. It was like Jim Eton, an empty husk. Dead to him. Like the Army was now dead to him. Funny to think that way about family, he thought. There was his blood family. His foster family. Military family. Each had taken care of him until, for whatever reason, it was time to move on.

He was leaving Iraq but not the war. He knew none of them really were. Their lives would forever be defined by having participated in it. Their service had given them everything they'd wanted: redemption, transformation, pride, or simply a brief respite from the mundane. And then it destroyed a part of them. Chandler would think about that many times in later years. After Gibson was killed in the accident and Witkowski sentenced to prison and Vogel moved to Alaska and was never heard from again. After the market crashed, Judy Eton sold the grocery to Buggman, whose father loaned him the money to snap up property, and Chandler left college and returned to the lake to manage the store. Only after his daughter was born did he cease trying to make real sense of what he'd seen and what he'd done. Of what could've been with Parker. And all the moments he wished had been different. His memories of Iraq or Afghanistan did not fade with time. Nor did his guilt at having survived. He only became better at pretending he was better, because that's what the people in his life demanded of him, until finally the weight of the experience became no different than the shards of shrapnel forever embedded in his legs and his feet. Tiny fragments deep beneath the skin, painful, irritating, inconvenient.

The plane climbed for a long time and finally leveled off. Vogel tipped sideways and fell onto Chandler's shoulder. His mouth hung open. His eyes were half closed and he was in a deep sleep.

"Absolutely," Chandler said. "A helluva thing."

The plane banked and flew south. Far below, the nighttime wind swept across the desert.

ACKNOWLEDGMENTS

I owe a massive debt to so many people for their help with this book. My agent, Kevin O'Connor, who took a chance on a rookie writer and didn't quit until the novel found a home. Victoria Barrett, editor and publisher of Engine Books, whose instincts and insight pulled this project across the finish line. My instructors and classmates at Northwestern University: Stuart Dybek, John Keene, Shauna Seliy, Naeem Murr, Patrick Somerville, Reginald Gibbons, Alex Higley, Yliana Gonzalez, Myra Thompson, Tedd Hawks, Rachel Curry, Whitney Youngs, and many, many others. My little chap, Milo, for whom I hope this book serves as proof to never give up on your crazy dreams. And last, but absolutley not least, my wife, Sarah, who read and reread these early pages when they were garbage, told me they were garbage, and busted my can until I finally got it right.

ABOUT THE AUTHOR

author photo by Robb Davidson

Adam Kovac served in the U.S. Army infantry, with deployments to Panama, Haiti, Iraq and Afghanistan. A former journalist, he's also covered the crime and court beats for newspapers in Indiana, Florida and Illinois. He lives in the Chicago suburbs with his wife and son.

CPSIA information can be obtained
at www.ICGtesting.com
Printed in the USA
BVHW080316141218
535593BV00003B/127/P